"You'd never get drunk on passion, would you, Nicole?"

Nicole shrugged. "I wouldn't care for the hangover that's sure to follow." She placed her drink on the table. "I believe in moderation at all times."

"Such a sensible woman!" Laughing, Greg lightly placed his hand on the back of her neck.

His fingers were chilled from his glass, and his touch made her shiver. She leaned away from it.

Greg laughed again. "I was hoping you'd choose to stay at a cottage, too."

Nicole arched an eyebrow. "You're staying at one of the cottages?"

"The one right next to yours, sweetheart. So if you hear anything go bump in the night, you can just call out my name."

"How comforting."

"It doesn't matter that you don't trust me, you know." He leaned closer to her. She could feel the heat emanating from him, could inhale his heady, masculine scent. "You'll still call out my name when you need me, Nicole."

Dear Reader,

Welcome to the Silhouette **Special Edition** experience! With your search for consistently satisfying reading in mind, every month the authors and editors of Silhouette **Special Edition** aim to offer you a stimulating blend of deep emotions and high romance.

The name Silhouette **Special Edition** and the distinctive arch on the cover represent a commitment—a commitment to bring you six sensitive, substantial novels each month. In the pages of a Silhouette **Special Edition**, compelling true-to-life characters face riveting emotional issues—and come out winners. Both celebrated authors and newcomers to the series strive for depth and dimension, vividness and warmth, in writing these stories of living and loving in today's world.

The result, we hope, is romance you can believe in. Deeply emotional, richly romantic, infinitely rewarding—that's the Silhouette **Special Edition** experience. Come share it with us—six times a month!

From all the authors and editors of Silhouette **Special Edition**,

Best wishes,

Leslie Kazanjian,
Senior Editor

BEVLYN MARSHALL
Treasure Deep

Silhouette Special Edition

Published by Silhouette Books New York

America's Publisher of Contemporary Romance

Books by Bevlyn Marshall

Silhouette Special Edition

Lonely at the Top #407
The Pride of His Life #441
Grady's Lady #506
Radio Daze #544
Goddess of Joy #562
Treasure Deep #598

BEVLYN MARSHALL,

a Connecticut resident, has had a varied career in fashion, public relations and marketing but finds writing the most challenging and satisfying occupation. When she's not at her typewriter, she enjoys tennis, needlepoint, long walks with her husband and toy spaniel, and reading. She believes that people who read are rarely bored or lonely because "the private pleasure of a good book is one of life's most rewarding pastimes."

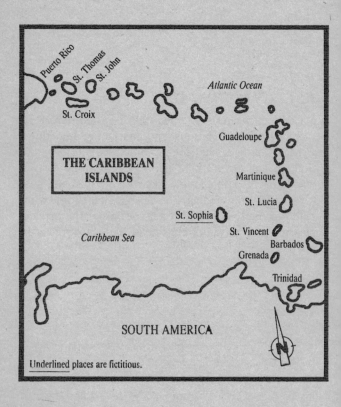

Puerto Rico

St. Thomas

St. John

St. Croix

Atlantic Ocean

Guadeloupe

**THE CARIBBEAN
ISLANDS**

Martinique

St. Lucia

St. Sophia

St. Vincent

Barbados

Caribbean Sea

Grenada

Trinidad

SOUTH AMERICA

N

Underlined places are fictitious.

Chapter One

"Not one inch higher, mister," Nicole Webster muttered under her breath to the man kneeling before her. He was sliding a frilly blue garter up her thigh.

Gregory Chase glanced up and winked at Nicole. "I guess I got carried away by the view. You've got beautiful legs, lady."

"Thank you," she said without smiling and dropped the skirt of her pink, ruffled maid of honor gown. She felt foolish performing this silly ritual in front of the wedding guests as the band played insinuating music in the background. She hadn't intended to catch the bridal bouquet, but her Aunt Jane had thrown it right at her. The groom, Toby Breck, had tossed Jane's garter to Chase, his best man.

Chase stood and towered over Nicole. Tall herself, she wasn't used to men towering over her. She had to tilt her chin up to look him straight in the eye. His eyes were a disconcerting sea green. Not that she was going to let them disconcert her. The sooner they played out this obligatory performance, the better. Nicole disliked being the center of attention. She much preferred observing others to being observed herself. That was one of the reasons she'd chosen research anthropology as her profession.

"Now we have to lead off the dance," she told Chase, placing her gloved hand on the broad ledge of his shoulder.

He lightly cupped her waist with his palm. "You don't look too thrilled about it, Nickie."

Nobody called her Nickie, but Nicole didn't correct him. "I'm not much of a dancer," she said.

"Just follow my lead." He moved his hand to the small of her back and pressed her closer.

It surprised Nicole that her body meshed so comfortably, so naturally with this stranger's. She fell into step with him as the band droned out "Moon River" in a slow, steady waltz beat.

"You lied," he said.

"What?" Startled, she pulled back to look at him.

"When you said you weren't much of a dancer. You're a natural. I knew you would be. You've got ballerina legs."

Nicole wished he'd stop complimenting her. She didn't trust Chase, although they'd only met a few hours ago, right before the wedding ceremony, and hadn't exchanged more than a sentence or two until now. It occurred to her that she might be judging him unfairly by association.

"How long have you known Toby Breck?" she asked him.

"Since he was born. Toby's my cousin."

Nicole filed that fact away in her precise, orderly mind and tried to gather more information about her aunt's new husband. "Did you grow up with Toby?"

Chase nodded.

"And where was that?"

"Lincoln, Nebraska."

"Oh, really? I thought Jane said that Toby came from Arizona."

"Originally. But after his mother died, his father moved to Nebraska to go into business with mine."

"What business was that?"

"Trucking."

Nicole frowned. "Trucking? But Toby told Jane that his father was a geophysicist investigating earthquake tremors in India, of all places. That's why he couldn't attend the wedding." Breck's excuse sounded even more outlandish to her now.

"At least I'm here to represent the family," Chase said easily. "I wouldn't have missed this wedding for the world. Jane's the best thing that could have happened to Toby."

That was no doubt true, Nicole thought. Jane had met Toby Breck on the Caribbean island of Saint Sophia when she'd taken a trip there with her Audubon group last month. Apparently Jane had forgotten all about bird-watching when the personable blond bartender at the inn began courting her. The question that hung heavy in Nicole's mind was if Breck had known about Jane's sudden wealth at the time. It would have been easy enough for him to have found out, since all of Jane's Audubon friends knew that she'd won a three-million-dollar sweepstakes ten weeks ago.

"I was stunned when my aunt told me she was getting married," she said to Chase. "It all happened so quickly."

"Yeah, a real whirlwind courtship." Chase spun her around a few times.

Other couples joined them on the dance floor, and Nicole observed how Chase stood out in this crowd of winter-pale Vermonters because of his height and deep tan. Because of his exceptional good looks, too, she had to admit. Not that she could fall under the spell of a handsome man as easily as her aunt had. Oh, no. Never again. Nicole had made that mistake when she was still in college, and she prided herself on learning from her mistakes. She felt the pressure of Chase's hand against her back but ignored his silent invitation to move closer.

"Don't you own the inn where Jane met Toby?" she asked him.

"That's right. The Sea Rover."

"It must have been difficult for you to get away."

"Not at all."

"But isn't winter the busy season in the Caribbean?"

"Saint Sophia's off the beaten tourist path and my inn's never that busy, no matter what the season. Which is fine with me."

His cavalier attitude bothered Nicole. "Don't you want your business to be a success?"

"Not really. Then I wouldn't have time for my real interest."

"Which is?" Getting information out of this man was like pulling teeth, she thought irritably.

Chase leaned forward to whisper in her ear. "Treasure."

His warm breath sent a shiver up Nicole's rigid spine. "What are you, a treasure hunter?"

"That's right, Nickie." He flashed a grin, and his deep tan made his strong, even teeth look even whiter and brighter. "Sunken treasure. I'm searching for one particular galleon that I'm sure was lost off the coast of Saint Sophia. I've been searching for five years."

"And you still haven't found it?"

"Not yet. But I will eventually," he replied with supreme confidence.

Then, without warning, he bent her in a dip that almost made her lose her balance. But his arms were a solid support, and he guided her right back into step with him.

"Sounds like a pretty risky enterprise to me," Nicole said a bit testily. She didn't like to be put off balance like that. "You could search forever and still end up with nothing."

Chase laughed. "Adventurers don't think like that. We're perpetual optimists."

Or opportunists, Nicole thought. "How can you support this venture of yours if your inn doesn't make any money?"

"Oh, I get by just fine," he assured her.

She believed him on that score, anyway.

"Enough about me," he said. "I want to hear all about you, Nickie. Your aunt mentioned that you wrote a brainy book about sex."

"About courting and mating practices throughout civilization," Nicole corrected stiffly.

Chase raised an eyebrow. "How romantic."

"Not romantic in the least," Nicole countered. "That was the whole point of the book. Most courting customs can be traced to primitive ritual. Dancing, for instance, has always been a part of marriage ceremonies. People danced to call the spirits to witness and bless the occasion."

"Then let's get into the spirit of it ourselves," Chase suggested. He dipped her low once more.

"I wish you'd stop doing that," she said a bit breathlessly when she was upright again.

"Oh, loosen up a little, Nickie." Chase gave her waist a squeeze. "Weddings are supposed to be fun. At least pretend you're having a good time for your aunt's sake."

"I'm not very good at pretending."

"That's for sure." His smile faded. "You don't approve of Toby, do you? You think Jane made a big mistake marrying him."

Nicole couldn't deny it. But she didn't want to admit it, either. "I barely know your cousin, Chase," she hedged. "So it wouldn't be fair to form an opinion about him."

"Yet you have," he insisted.

"Listen, all I want is for my aunt to be happy," Nicole replied, aware that there was a catch in her voice. "She has all my best wishes, I assure you."

"And I assure *you* that Toby has a good heart and a fine character."

"Spoken like a true best man," Nicole said sardonically. "Did you know that originally the best man's chief duty was to help his friend capture a bride by force? He was chosen for being strong, brave and fearless.''

"Sounds like me all right."

Nicole ignored his playful boast. "Once the barbaric deed was done," she continued, "the best man acted as an envoy for the groom and went to the poor girl's distraught family with gifts to try to appease them. Sometimes they accepted the gifts." She paused. "And sometimes they tortured and killed him."

Chase grinned. "Well, luckily times have changed. I do have a gift that I'd like to offer to the bride's niece, though."

Nicole narrowed her eyes. "What sort of gift?"

"Friendship."

"Why should *we* be friends, Chase?" She didn't mean to sound rude, but she was suspicious of this self-proclaimed adventurer.

"Because we both care about Jane," he answered softly.

"I certainly do. But you barely know her."

"I know enough about the lady to admire and respect her. And I know she makes my cousin happy."

And no doubt you also know she has three million dollars sitting in the bank, Nicole silently added.

"Give Toby a chance," Chase continued. "Once you get to know him, you'll like him. And don't worry about the age difference between him and your aunt. From the moment they met, they were on the same wavelength. I saw it happen. It was love at first sight."

Nicole rolled her gray eyes. "That concept is a myth from the early Greeks, Chase. They believed that every man and woman on earth began as one element, but then some great power divided them into two separate beings. Legend had it that if you were fortunate enough to find your other half again, you were struck by love at first sight.''

"Don't you believe in such a thing ever happening, Nickie?''

"Well, *attraction* at first sight, perhaps," she replied in the cool lecture voice she'd perfected. "We're all predisposed to be attracted to certain types." Such as tall, dark men with green eyes, she thought. She'd recognized this predisposition in herself the first moment she'd set eyes on Gregory Chase. She'd been smart enough to disregard it, too. "But there's no such person as your one and only other half, Chase," she concluded forcefully.

"You're kidding?" He pretended to look shocked. "Next thing you'll be telling me is that there's no such person as Santa Claus, either."

"A legend that began in Asia Minor in the fourth century," Nicole informed him. "And the Easter Bunny probably originated from pre-Christian fertility rites. Hence its otherwise inexplicable association with eggs."

He pressed his long, hard body against hers and moved rhythmically, erotically. "Dance has always been part of ancient fertility rites, hasn't it, Nickie?"

He was teasing her, she knew. Still, her body responded to his—with a jolt of excitement in the pit of her stomach. She pushed away from him, politely but firmly. "Excuse me, but I don't care to dance anymore. My feet hurt." With that, she proceeded to march off the floor without looking back at him.

Greg Chase watched her retreat with an amused expression. From what he could make out of her lithe, lean figure through the camouflage of pink ruffles, he surmised that she would look terrific in a bikini. He imagined her wearing the smallest one possible, laughing and playing in the waves on his Caribbean island. Did she ever laugh? he wondered. Was she ever playful? Or was she always uptight and aloof? An ice queen, he thought—blond, cool, elegant and distant. He went off to the open bar to get her a glass of champagne. Maybe that would warm her up a bit. He doubted it, though. It would take a lot more than a glass of champagne to thaw Nicole Webster.

Nicole glanced around the crowded hall for her aunt and spotted Jane in the distance, her arm linked with Toby's as they chatted with some of the guests. People often remarked on the close physical resemblance between aunt and niece, but now Nicole was aware that she looked tense and worried, while Jane's expression was joyous as she gazed up at her husband. How innocent and trusting she looked, Nicole mused. Even though she was fourteen years younger than her aunt, Nicole felt protective toward her. At forty, Jane had seen little of the world. She'd lived in the small town of Jasper, Vermont all her life, devoted to her invalid mother.

And now she was marrying a man she'd known for only a month! How Nicole wished that she'd had the chance to have a long heart-to-heart talk with Jane before the wedding. Not that she would have tried to talk her out of marrying Toby. But she would have cautioned her to wait awhile.

She doubted Jane would have taken her advice, though. Her aunt had been determined to marry Toby Breck as soon as possible. In fact, Nicole had only arrived at the wedding in the nick of time. She'd been on a lecture tour when she'd received Jane's call announcing her wedding plans, and had completed her last engagement just yesterday. She'd flown into Boston from Chicago last night, and she and her father had driven to Vermont this morning. The only private time she'd had with her aunt was when they'd dressed for the ceremony, and it had been far too late to caution Jane to wait then.

Now Nicole watched her aunt throw back her head and laugh with delight at something Toby had said. *Please don't let her get hurt,* she prayed, hoping with all her heart that this prayer was not in vain. She sighed deeply as doubt crowded out hope with a heavy insistence.

"Was that sigh for me, Nickie?"

Chase's deep voice startled Nicole, and she turned to him with a quick intake of breath. "No, it wasn't for you," she said.

His wide mouth turned up at the corners. "Don't you ever flirt, lady?"

"Flirts were hardly considered ladies when the word came into the English language during the sixteenth century," she replied. "A flirt was considered a hussy. Of course, Eibl-Eibesfeld points out that a woman's impulse to flirt could stem from the primordial flight or fight response. It's a behavior that can be observed in many cultures and—"

"Here." Greg interrupted, handing her a glass of champagne.

Nicole realized that she'd been chattering on. She tended to talk too much when she felt uncomfortable, and Gregory Chase made her feel terribly uncomfortable. "I'm boring you, aren't I?"

"Not at all," he said. "I just figured you needed to wet your whistle before your continued your discourse."

"Don't worry. I've completed it," she said, accepting the glass.

"To Toby and Jane," he toasted, raising his. "May they live happily ever after."

Nicole didn't believe in fairy tales, but if anyone deserved a happy future, she felt her aunt certainly did. Determined to keep her reservations about Toby to herself, since expressing them would do absolutely no good now and probably never would have, she drank to the couple. Still, the bubbly liquid tasted bitter to her.

"You're a hard woman to please," Greg said, watching her closely. "You don't even like champagne!"

"What makes you say that?"

"That funny face you made when you swallowed it down."

"I meant, what makes you think I'm a hard woman to please?"

"Well, for one thing, you don't seem to find my company especially pleasing."

"Meaning most women do?"

Greg shrugged. "Some do."

"No need to be modest, Chase," Nicole told him. "I've made a study of ideal courting faces and bodies and yours conforms to the archetype that females have been programmed to find appealing for centuries.''

"You don't say?'' Greg did his best to look suitably impressed. "Well, lucky me!''

"Indeed,'' Nicole agreed blandly. "In a more primitive society you would probably be head of the tribe and have an impressive collection of wives.''

Greg shook his dark head. "Not me. I'm a one-woman man.''

"Man is not by nature monogamous,'' Nicole stated. She hadn't learned that from a textbook. She'd learned it the hard way. She slipped off one pink satin shoe and wiggled her cramped toes.

Greg glimpsed the stocking-sheathed foot peeking out beneath the hem of her gown and found it interesting that Nicole's toenails were painted bright red, although her fingernails were unvarnished. Perhaps she was a secret hedonist. It would be even more interesting to find out.

"Let's go sit down,'' he suggested. She slipped her foot into her shoe and didn't object when he took her arm and guided her through the crowd to an unoccupied table.

"Take off your shoes and put your feet in my lap,'' he told her the moment they sat down.

Nicole looked at him askance. "I beg your pardon?''

"Didn't you say your feet hurt?'' he asked. "I'll massage them for you. Don't worry, no one will be able to see what I'm doing to you under the table.''

"You make it sound so...'' Color rose to her cheeks. "So lascivious.''

It amused him to see her blush. "Come on," he urged, patting his lap. "Don't be so damn prim."

Nicole kicked off her shoes and complied, much to her own amazement. Perhaps it was the challenge in his teasing green eyes. "You're on, Chase. Do with my feet what you will."

He proceeded to do marvelous things to them with his big, clever hands—stroking and kneading until Nicole's toes turned up in pleasure. "This is really very nice of you, Chase," she said in a husky voice that didn't sound at all like her normal one. "Have you had professional experience as a masseur?"

"Not professional," he replied. "But I have had a certain amount of experience."

Nicole could well imagine how practiced Chase was in giving women pleasure. No! She would not allow herself to imagine that at all. She would make polite conversation with him instead. "I don't usually wear high heels," she said. "I prefer sensible shoes, but I didn't think Jane would appreciate her maid of honor stomping down the church aisle in a pair of sneakers."

"No, I guess that wouldn't have been in keeping with tradition."

"But it's such a ridiculous tradition! Women wearing high heels, I mean. It all started during the seventeenth century, you know."

In fact, Greg did know that, but he didn't interrupt her.

"The French court popularized raised heels," she continued. "Partly for practical reasons. Streets were rather mucky in those days, and elevated shoes kept the aristocrats' feet out of the mud."

"Makes sense to me," Greg said. He glided his palm up Nicole's sleek calf, but she shifted uncomfortably. Skittish, he thought, and lowered his hand to her foot again.

"But it doesn't make sense in this day and age," she went on. "High heels are uncomfortable and impractical, but women continue to wear them because men find them so attractive." She shook her head over the silliness of it.

"A guy could learn a hell of a lot hanging around you, Nickie."

She was sure she heard mockery in his voice and swung her legs off his. "Thanks for the massage," she said, putting her shoes back on. "That was above and beyond the best man's duties."

"Not this best man, sweetheart." His bold eyes glinted with humor. "Are you going to run away from me again?"

"I'm not running away," she denied emphatically. "But I'd like to have a few minutes alone with my aunt before she leaves on her honeymoon. Did you know that in ancient times the maid of honor's duty was to stay close by the bride to protect her from evil demons, Chase?"

"Is that right?" He gave her his slow, lazy grin. "And do you think you managed to do that today, Nickie?"

"Time will tell." Nicole stood up abruptly. "Excuse me. I'm going to find Jane."

Chapter Two

Greg continued to smile as he watched Nicole walk away, her back ramrod straight. A veritable walking encyclopedia, he thought. He wondered how much time it would take him to break down her defenses. A lot more time than he could spare, he decided. He couldn't let himself get sidetracked now. Besides, Nicole Webster had made it clear that her interest in romance was strictly academic. Greg chuckled to himself. At least her *feet* had been putty in his hands for a while.

"What's so funny, Greg?" Toby Breck flopped into the chair that Nicole had vacated.

Greg's smile had immediately faded. "Since when is your old man a geophysicist, Tobias?"

Breck shifted uncomfortably. "I had to make up some kind of story to explain why he couldn't be here today."

"You could have told Jane the truth," Greg said, his voice low and even.

"Yeah, right. She would have been delighted to hear that the man she was about to marry had a father in prison."

"Don't underestimate Jane's love for you, buddy."

"I didn't want to push my luck, okay?"

"No, it's not okay, dammit!" Greg thumped his fist on the table but didn't raise his voice. "Why'd you have to go and tell such a preposterous lie? And to make matters worse, you didn't even clue me in on it."

"Did you cover for me, Greg?"

He nodded, the muscles in his lean face tight. "But I don't like it, Toby."

"I'll tell Jane the truth eventually," Breck said.

"You'd better, because that niece of hers is going to sniff it out herself if you don't." Greg's eyes drifted through the crowd as he tried to locate a particular shade of pink in the sea of colors. But he'd lost sight of Nicole and turned his attention back to Toby. "The one thing you don't want to risk losing is Jane's trust in you. If you do, it'll ruin everything."

"I won't, Greg. I'm going to make this work."

"You'd better," Greg replied, shaking his finger at Toby. "Or you'll be plenty sorry."

Standing by her aunt, Nicole observed Chase and Breck conversing and wished that she could read lips. Being a trained observer, though, she interpreted the body language and facial expressions the two men exhibited and inferred that Chase had been reproving Breck about something. And then warning or perhaps threatening him. Obviously, Chase was the stronger of the two.

"Isn't he the cutest, sweetest, most adorable man?" Jane asked as she followed her niece's intent gaze.

Those were hardly words that Nicole would have used to describe Gregory Chase, but then she realized that Jane was referring to her husband, of course. She stopped staring at the two men and gave her aunt a forced smile.

"Yes, adorable," she replied. There could be no denying that about Toby Breck. His upturned nose, flaxen hair and ingratiating smile gave him an air of innocence that made him look even younger than thirty.

"I wish there was time for you to get to know him better before we left, dear," Jane said. Her gentle blue eyes lighted up. "Here's an idea! Join us in Saint Sophia, Nicole. You could use the vacation. You seem a little tense to me."

Nicole gave a hollow laugh. "You don't really want me barging in on your honeymoon, do you?"

"Our whole life together is going to be a honeymoon," Jane replied dreamily.

Nicole took her aunt's hand. "When you come back from the Caribbean, why don't you and Toby spend some time with me in Boston?"

"But we're not coming back, dear."

"I don't understand. I thought you'd be returning home in a few weeks."

"My home is where my husband is now, Nicole. Toby prefers living in Saint Sophia. He can't take the cold weather. Poor darling, he's been shivering ever since he arrived in Vermont.''

"But you can't just up and leave your whole life behind.''

"Can't I?'' Jane smiled softly. "I think it's time I did exactly that. Not that I regret all the years I spent taking care of Mother. But now that she's gone to her final reward, I want to start a new life. With Toby. I want to run barefoot in the sand with him every day, not trudge through the snow all alone.''

"Why did you keep your plans a secret from me until now?'' Nicole asked her aunt, trying to keep the hurt out of her voice.

"I just made up my mind a few hours ago, dear.''

"Did Toby pressure you into this decision?''

"Not at all! Even though he can't stand the climate, he was perfectly willing to move to Vermont if that's what I wanted. But I decided it made more sense to live in Saint Sophia after discussing it with Gregory.''

"Chase influenced you?'' Nicole didn't like the sound of that one bit.

"He merely suggested that Toby and I should consider his inn our home. Wasn't that generous of him?''

"I doubt generosity had anything to do with it.''

Jane looked surprised. "What do you mean by that, dear?''

Nicole wasn't quite sure what she meant, but felt that she could at least caution her aunt about Chase, if not Toby. "There's something about that man that makes me suspicious,'' she said.

"Excuse me for interrupting such a serious discussion, ladies.''

Nicole and Jane turned to see Gregory Chase looming over them. Nicole wondered how much of the conversation he'd overheard.

"Actually, my aunt and I were talking about you," she said coolly.

"Is that right?" His eyes held hers for a moment. "Well, I'm flattered."

"What makes you think we were saying anything flattering?"

Jane cleared her throat and squeezed her niece's hand, as she often had when Nicole was a child and had been too outspoken. "I've been trying to convince Nicole to come to Saint Sophia, Gregory. Maybe you can help me persuade her."

"Oh, I don't think anybody could persuade Nickie to do anything she doesn't want to." Greg pierced Nicole with his sharp green gaze again.

"You're right about that," she told him. But it wasn't lost on her that he'd avoided extending an invitation.

Toby joined them and kissed the top of Jane's head, brushing his cheek against the spray of lilies of the valley interwoven in her chignon. "Have you missed me during the last five minutes?" he asked her.

"Every second," she assured him.

He tugged at his bow tie. "I can't wait to get out of this monkey suit."

Jane shook her head indulgently. "You're always so in a hurry to get out of civilized clothes, honey."

"Only when you're around, bunny."

Nicole saw her mature aunt instantaneously change into a giggling schoolgirl. She looked away, embarrassed.

Greg checked his watch. "You two lovebirds had better leave soon if you want to make that flight out of New York."

"Have you said all your goodbyes, Mrs. Breck?" Toby asked his bride.

"All but the most difficult one." Jane turned to Nicole. "You'll write to me, won't you, dear?"

"Of course I will."

Jane hugged her hard. "Promise you'll come to Saint Sophia as soon as you have some free time."

"I promise," Nicole said, although free time was a luxury she rarely indulged in.

They hugged again, and then Toby gently but firmly drew Jane away. "We can't miss that plane, bunny," he said.

Nicole and Greg, along with many of the wedding guests, followed the departing couple outside, where a limousine, decorated with blue and pink streamers, waited. It had begun to snow and the white flakes mingled with the bright confetti people tossed at Jane and Toby as they ran to the car. Nicole wondered how many of them realized that they were enacting a pagan rite of showering newlyweds with rice, wheat or nuts to ensure a fruitful union.

She blew a kiss to her aunt. "Good luck, Jane," she whispered as the car drove away. She felt a large, warm hand on her back.

"You needn't look so sad, Nickie," Greg said. "You haven't lost an aunt, you've gained an uncle."

Nicole found it absurd to regard vacuous Toby Breck, less than five years older than herself, as an uncle, and she could tell from Chase's amused expression that he considered it just as absurd. But unlike him, Nicole found nothing amusing about it.

"I'm going to miss Jane," she said. "I hope she changes her mind about making Saint Sophia her home and comes back to Vermont."

"Without Toby?"

"I didn't say that, Chase."

"But you were thinking it."

"That's not true," Nicole protested. "For better or worse, Toby's her husband now." That hadn't come out right, she thought. "I mean, I respect the institution of marriage. It's the backbone of modern civilization."

Greg laughed. "You're no doubt the most unromantic woman I've ever encountered, Nicole Webster." He took off his jacket and draped it over her shoulders. "Why don't you let me try romancing you for the next few days? I'll give it my best effort, I assure you."

She noticed how the snowflakes shone like diamonds in his dark hair and caught in his thick black lashes. She hated to admit it to herself, but she knew that she would feel more comfortable with this stranger if he wasn't so devastatingly handsome. "Aren't you going back to Saint Sophia today, too, Chase?"

"No. I want to give Toby and Jane some time alone at the inn, so I thought I'd take the opportunity to go skiing while I'm in Vermont. Do you ski, Nickie?"

"I haven't for years. And I was never very good at it."

"That's what you said about dancing," Greg reminded her. "I guess it all depends on your partner.

Come skiing with me tomorrow, Nickie. We'll have a good time together.''

She was tempted by his invitation, but only for a moment. "I can't. I'm leaving for Boston in the morning."

"Couldn't you leave in the evening instead?"

"No, I have work to do."

"But tomorrow's Sunday."

"Libraries are open on Sunday and I want to do some research for my next book. Thanks for the offer, though."

He brushed snow off the sleeves of his formal white shirt. "I forgot how cold it gets up north. I'm not used to it."

He'd managed to make Nicole feel a twinge of guilt. "Why don't you join my father and me for dinner this evening?" she asked, trying to sound more hospitable. "We're spending the night at Jane's house. Before you accept, I'd better warn you that I'm doing the cooking. My specialty is scrambled eggs, because I never mastered the art of making an omelet."

He grinned. "Sounds good to me, Nickie. I'm staying at the Bear and Elk. How do I get to Jane's house from there?"

She gave him directions. "Seven o'clock," she said. She slipped off his jacket and handed it back to him before running back inside.

"I wish you hadn't invited him, Nicole." Alex Webster kept his eyes straight ahead as he drove away from the reception hall with his daughter. "I'm in no mood to entertain some stranger tonight. We know even less about Chase than we do about Breck. Which is a big fat nothing!''

"That's exactly the reason I asked him to dinner," Nicole replied patiently. "To learn more about Toby." Not that she would mind learning more about Greg Chase at the same time.

Her father sniffed. "Why should we believe anything Chase tells us? He's no doubt a con artist, same as his cousin."

"That's not fair, Dad. Didn't you always caution me to avoid making rash assumptions about people?" Her father, a scientist, had taught Nicole that conclusions should be made through observation and classification of established facts, not intuition and suspicion. But Nicole had seen the tears in her father's eyes as he'd escorted Jane down the church aisle that morning and knew that his own objectivity had been displaced by concern for his "baby" sister.

"You're right, Nicole," he said after a moment. "We need more information. I fully intend to give this Chase fellow the third degree during dinner."

The third degree! Nicole smiled at the idea of her mild father intimidating the likes of Greg Chase. "Stop at Abe's," she said, pointing to a country store up ahead. "We need groceries, and maybe I can pick up some truth serum to slip into Chase's salad dressing."

"Actually, there's no such thing," her father commented. "An anesthesiologist named House described the drug scopolamine as a truth serum back in the 1920s, but his claim that it could induce people to tell the truth was never medically justified."

As she listened to her father, it occurred to Nicole that she often sounded just like him. They were both more comfortable dealing with facts rather than emotions. Growing up, she'd deliberately modeled herself on him rather than her mother. As far as Nicole was concerned, her mother was a flighty, foolish woman who hurt others in her blind pursuit of romantic love. She'd left Boston when Nicole was four to follow the new love of her life to Europe. Since the divorce, Nicole's father had remained single, but her mother had remarried three times. Nicole found it sadly ironic that her mother's name was Prudence.

Her father parked in front of the store, and Nicole promised him that her grocery shopping would take less than five minutes. They both checked their watches after she stated this.

While Nicole entered the little market, the elderly proprietor gave her a curt nod in greeting. "Long time no see," he said. "Hear tell your aunt tied the knot today. About time."

"It was a lovely wedding," Nicole replied sweetly. Having spent many childhood vacations at her aunt's home, she was used to Abe's tactless manner.

"Everybody in Jasper's talking about it, you know," he informed her. "Biggest news we had hereabouts since Jane won that sweepstakes. Up and married some beachboy bartender, did she?"

Nicole wished she could refute this, but as far as she knew, Abe's description of Toby Breck was quite accurate. Rather than answer his question, she asked him for a dozen fresh eggs.

"Laid this very morning," he assured her, placing the carton on the counter. "So when are you going to get yourself hitched, Nicole?"

"When you finally pop the question to me, Abel."

He made a wheezing sound that Nicole recognized as his version of a laugh. "A pretty thing like you, I bet you got more suitors than you can shake a stick at down in Boston."

"You bet. I've got to fight them off with that stick."

"Don't fight them off too long," he advised, narrowing his beady eyes. "How old are you now, anyways, Nicole? Twenty-three or four?"

"Twenty-six, actually."

He whistled. "No spring chicken! In my day that would have been considered an old maid. Whatever happened to that young fellow you brought to Jasper to meet your aunt a few years back? Had a beard and needed a haircut, as I recall. You sure seemed real smitten with that one."

The fading image of Miles Avery floated to the surface of Nicole's memory. "A case of temporary insanity," she replied dryly. "I'm in a bit of a rush, Abe. My father's waiting in the car. Maybe we can chat about my love life some other time, okay?"

Abe nodded. "I get the hint, young lady. I'll mind my own beeswax. Let me cut you off a chunk of cheddar on the house."

Nicole's father carried the bag of groceries into the old-fashioned kitchen and placed it on the wooden counter. He turned to his daughter with a wistful smile. "I spent many a happy day in this old kitchen as a boy," he said. "Of course, my mother still had her health then."

"I wish I'd known Grandma before she became so ill," Nicole said, unpacking the groceries. "For as long as I can remember she was bedridden. She never came downstairs. Aunt Jane used to serve her all her meals on a tray and cater to her every whim. She was always so even-tempered with Grandma. I did my best to follow her example during my visits here, but I could never be as patient. Grandma could be very demanding."

"That's for sure," Alex agreed. "It couldn't have been easy for Jane. She was only seventeen when our father died, and Mother was never the same after that." He tapped his finger against his temple.

Although he'd never come right out and told Nicole that her grandmother had become an unbalanced hypochondriac, she'd guessed it by the time she was twelve. "Aunt Jane certainly had her hands full," she said.

Her father sighed. "I feel guilty about that, Nicole. I'd left home years before and never fully appreciated my sister's burden. I was too involved in my work at the lab."

"I don't think Jane ever considered Grandma a burden, Dad," Nicole corrected gently. "She loved her very much and was devoted to her."

"But Jane sacrificed so much! She should have married and left home, rather than waste the best years of her life without a husband."

Nicole shook her head. "Oh, Dad, what a chauvinistic thing to say. Jane didn't need a husband to have a satisfying life. She enjoyed her job at the animal shelter, and she had lots of friends and outside interests. I always admired her for that, you know. For not needing a man in her life to make it complete."

"Well, she's got one in it now, doesn't she?" Alex's tone was doleful.

Nicole turned away to put the eggs and cream in the refrigerator, noting that her aunt had left it defrosted and spotless. "Did Jane tell you that she has no intention of returning to Vermont after her honeymoon, Dad?"

He groaned. "She dropped that bomb on me in the middle of her wedding reception. She's making a big mistake. But I'm hoping she'll get bored in Saint Sophia. Get bored of that Huck Finn impostor she now calls her husband, I mean. I give that marriage six months at the most."

"Dad! That doesn't sound like you. Or Jane. She wouldn't take her vows so lightly. She's not like..." Nicole stopped herself.

"Like your mother?" Alex asked wryly. "You're right. Jane is nothing like Prudence. And neither are you, thank God, Nicole. You're a sensible, rational young woman. By the time your mother was your age, she'd already left me and gone on to husband number two. What number is she on now? I've lost track through the years."

Nicole knew very well that he hadn't, so she didn't reply. Instead, she kissed his furrowed brow. "I'm going upstairs to change out of this gown. I can't imagine why Jane thought pink ruffles would suit me. But since that's what she selected, I wasn't going to protest."

Her father stepped back and examined her as carefully as he would a minute object under his microscope. "Actually, you look lovely," Alex pronounced. "Just like a fairy-tale princess." He winced. "What a silly thing to say."

If not silly, then certainly surprising, Nicole thought. Her father had always refused to read fairy tales to her when she was a child, claiming he didn't want to fill her head with nonsense. His fanciful, unexpected compliment touched her. He'd praised her intelligence many times before, but never her looks. She thanked him for it with another quick kiss before leaving the kitchen.

She took her overnight bag up to her aunt's bedroom and changed into a comfortable pair of slacks and a bulky sweater. Comfortable but not especially flattering, Nicole thought as she looked at herself in the long dressing-table mirror. She found herself wishing that she'd packed something prettier to wear, now that she'd invited Chase to dinner. She turned away from the mirror. Why should she care about impressing him?

Because she found him extremely attractive, of course. It would be foolish to deny that. Nicole never lied, especially to herself. Not that she intended to do anything about this attraction. All she wanted from Chase was information. Perhaps she should have accepted his invitation to go skiing the next day. She shook her head. There was no sense in getting too chummy with a man she didn't quite trust.

Besides, she really did have work to do in Boston. Her work was important to her, the most important thing in her life right now. She found it hard to believe that at one time she'd considered Miles Avery the most important thing in her life. Thank goodness she'd seen the light in time! Miles had turned out to be a huge, painful mistake, and Nicole had resolved that she would never allow herself to become so infatuated with a man again.

She looked around Jane's bedroom, taking in the familiar flowered wallpaper, the pink satin comforter, the graceful dressing table and bulky bureaus. The scent of Jane's tuberose and orange perfume still lingered in the air, and Nicole felt a deep, sudden loss. Jane had always been more like a sister than an aunt to her. She'd been her friend and confidante growing up.

Feeling depressed, she unpacked her bag and put it away in Jane's closet. All her winter clothes had been left behind, Nicole noted, along with her lovely cream velvet wedding dress. There was a note attached to it. Nicole unpinned it.

My Dearest Niece

Toby has given me exactly two minutes to change before we take the limo to the airport. He's always in such a rush! He leaves me breathless.

This gown is yours if you want it. It would give me such pleasure to see you wear it on your wedding day. Oh, I can imagine the frown on your face as you read that last sentence, dear! I know you have no intention of getting married. But neither had I until I met Toby. So we never know what the future holds, do we?

Anyway, if you decide not to keep my wedding dress, please donate it to some charitable organization, along with all the other clothes in my closet. I won't be needing them in balmy Saint Sophia.

This house is yours now, Nicole. My mother left it to me, and now I want you to have it as a retreat. But if you choose to sell it, that's fine with me, too.

The last thing I want to tell you, dear, is that I've never been happier in my entire life. Oh, dear! I hear Toby coming up the stairs to get me. And I haven't even dressed yet. Knowing him, he'll carry me out to the car as I am! He's such an impetuous fool and—

Jane's elegant handwriting broke off. But there was a printed scrawl on the bottom of the ecru stationery.

Don't worry, Nicole. Tempting as it is, I'm not going to carry Jane off in her skivvies. I don't want her to catch a cold. I intend to always take very good care of my preshus wife. I love her like crazy.

                              Best wishes, Toby.

Nicole disregarded Toby's bad penmanship and the misspelling, trying her best to believe the sentiments he expressed. Why was it so difficult for her to accept that he really did love Jane "like crazy?" Any man worthy of Jane would appreciate both her mature beauty and beautiful spirit. But was a man like Toby Breck worthy? The trouble was, Nicole didn't know what sort of man Breck was. She couldn't judge him.

But she couldn't help wishing that he had proposed to Jane *before* she'd won all that money.

She went downstairs and found her father in the living room, gazing at framed family photographs displayed on the mantel.

"Jane's high school yearbook picture," he said, picking one up. "It's hard to believe it was taken over twenty years ago."

"She hasn't changed much," Nicole said.

"Oh, we all change through the years," Alex replied wearily. "And Jane certainly must have to fall for the likes of Toby Breck. She used to be so discriminating. Why *him*, Nicole? After all these years, why did she finally choose a man like him?"

"It was her choice to make, Dad. And he seems devoted to her." Nicole gave him the note.

Alex quickly read it, frowning when he got to Toby's writing. "Words are cheap, Nicole. Especially misspelled ones." He handed her back the note. "I knew Jane was giving you the house, by the way. We discussed it at the reception. She's going to write to her lawyer to transfer the title to your name."

"I don't feel right about accepting it, Dad. This is your family home, not mine."

"Nonsense. You've spent more time in it than I have over the years. And I think Jane's correct. You could use a quiet place in the country. When's the last time you took a vacation?"

Nicole shrugged. "I don't enjoy vacations."

"Neither do I," Alex said. "A frivolous expenditure of precious time, as far as I'm concerned. What time is this Chase coming, by the way?"

"I told him to be here at seven," Nicole said. "He's staying at the Bear and Elk."

"That's where Breck supposedly spent last night, isn't it? At least Jane reserved a room for him there for propriety's sake. I certainly didn't appreciate the sight of him eating breakfast here when we arrived this morning."

Nicole noticed how the blood rushed to her father's face and spoke in a calming tone. "Where Toby spent the night is Jane's business, not ours, Dad."

"I know. I know. But I can't help thinking of her as my kid sister. I was ten when she was born. I taught her how to drink milk from a cup!"

Nicole patted his back to comfort him. "Jane's an adult now, Dad. She can take care of herself."

"Can she?" Alex locked eyes with his daughter.

She quickly looked away so that he wouldn't see his concern reflected in her own eyes. "I'd better see to dinner," she said and went off to the kitchen.

Chapter Three

At eight o'clock Nicole and her father were eating scrambled eggs and melted cheddar cheese sandwiches in the dining room. The place Nicole had set for Chase remained undisturbed.

"Maybe we should have waited a little bit longer for him," she said.

Alex snorted. "He's obviously not coming, Nicole. The least he could have done was call to tell us he wasn't."

"He might have gotten lost," Nicole suggested. "He's not familiar with this area and country roads can be confusing."

"You're grasping at straws now. Chase didn't strike me as a man who would lose his way. I got the impression that nothing could stop him from reaching any goal he set for himself."

"Yes, I got the same impression," Nicole said. An uneasiness fluttered through her. "He claims he's a treasure hunter, you know."

"Really? That hardly sounds like a legitimate profession."

Nicole nibbled at the edge of her sandwich. "Perhaps he was only teasing me."

Alex frowned. "Why would Chase want to do that?"

"Well, *I* don't know. But he seemed to enjoy provoking me."

"I think you should stay away from him."

Nicole glanced at the empty chair across from her. "I doubt I'll ever see him again."

Alex gave his daughter a close look. "Good. We already have a fortune hunter in the family. We don't need a treasure hunter in it, too."

"You're jumping to all sorts of conclusions, Dad," she said sharply. "Toby's given us no reason to believe that he doesn't love Jane for herself alone. And to suggest that Chase and I will ever get involved is absurd!"

"I'm sorry, Nicole." Her father stabbed at his scrambled eggs. "But I've found today a bit of a strain."

"So have I, Dad. I'm sorry, too. I didn't mean to snap at you like that."

"That's all right, my dear. We're both a little on edge."

As they shared a smile of fond understanding, the phone rang. "That must be Chase," Nicole said, leaping up from the table. Her heart leaped, too.

Her pulse rate leveled when the owner of the deep male voice identified himself as Chuck Dickens from the Bear and Elk Inn.

"I owe you an apology, Ms. Webster," he said. "A guest here, Mr. Chase, asked me to call you this afternoon. But then Keely—that's my wife—returned from the doctor's with some wonderful news and it completely slipped my mind." He laughed. "Twins! She's going to have twins! Well, I shouldn't be surprised. Keely always manages to do double of what's expected."

"Congratulations, Mr. Dickens," Nicole said with sincere enthusiasm. She'd never met him or his wife but she was delighted, anyway. She had a soft spot in her heart for babies. "And since Mr. Chase didn't show up for dinner tonight, I can guess what his message was. What I can't understand is why he didn't call and give it to me personally."

"Oh, he tried but no one answered."

That must have been while she was at the grocery store, Nicole surmised.

"He checked out in a big hurry," Mr. Dickens continued. "Said he had to make a flight out of New York this evening."

Nicole narrowed her eyes. "To the Caribbean?"

"I have no idea where he was going. Again, I apologize for the delay in relaying his message."

"It doesn't matter," Nicole assured the pleasant man.

"Do you possibly know Mr. Chase's mailing address?" he asked her.

"Why? Did he forget something?"

"Well, yes. He did." A pause. "He forgot to pay his bill. And Mr. Breck's, too, which he said he'd also take care of. Before he rushed off, he told me he'd left a check in his room, but it seems he forgot to."

"Oh, I'm sure that wasn't intentional," Nicole said. But she wasn't sure at all. "I'll tell you what, Mr. Dickens. I'll stop by the Bear and Elk tomorrow morning to pay for the rooms. And I assure you, I won't forget!" After congratulating him again on his expected twins, Nicole hung up and marched back to the dining room, eyes flashing.

"Was that Chase?" her father asked.

She sat down and took a deep, calming breath. "No, it was the proprietor of the Bear and Elk. He told me Chase took off without paying his bill. I promised to pay it myself tomorrow."

"Why should *you* make good his bad debt?"

"For Jane's sake," Nicole told her father. "Apparently, Chase promised to cover Toby's bill, too. And there's already enough gossip around here about Toby. I don't want the word chiseler added to his description."

Her father pulled back his shoulders. "Exactly how do the people in Jasper describe my sister's new husband, Nicole?"

"It's not even worth mentioning. And I shouldn't have. I didn't hear a word against Toby from the wedding guests today, Dad."

"But you must have heard something from somebody," he pressed. "Who?"

"Abe the grocer," she admitted. "But he never has a good word to say about anybody."

"What did he say about Breck?"

Nicole sighed. "Just that he was a beachboy bartender. It seems the Jasper ladies that accompanied Jane to Saint Sophia didn't waste time describing her romance to the rest of the town."

"That's the way it is in small towns, Nicole. Everybody knows everybody else's business." His shoulders slumped. "I'm more concerned than ever about Jane now. What sort of characters has she gotten involved with? What if Breck is as much of a scoundrel as his slippery cousin?"

"It's possible that Chase *forgot* to pay his bill."

"Possible but not probable, Nicole. What further proof do we need that the man is a swindler?"

"More than we have," she insisted.

They sat in silence for a moment, not touching their food.

"Why don't you admit that you're thinking the same thing I am?" her father finally suggested. "Those two men are going to try to con Jane out of her millions."

"Please, Dad. Don't talk that way," Nicole implored. "You've never cared about money and neither do I. Neither does Jane, for that matter."

"That's exactly the problem," he stated emphatically. "People like us don't stand a chance against those who care for nothing *but* money and will do anything to get it."

Chase's bright, dangerous smile flashed into Nicole's mind and she felt a sudden chill. "Eat your eggs, Dad. They're getting cold."

Alex pushed away his plate. "Do you know what Jane used to do with her allowance when she was a kid?" he asked.

"Probably donated it to needy causes," Nicole guessed.

"Not exactly. She'd buy birdseed with it. Jane couldn't bear the thought of birds going hungry in the winter."

Nicole smiled. "She hasn't changed much."

"I wish she had! Now I'm afraid a pair of vultures will get fat on her generosity." He threw down his napkin and stood up.

"There you go thinking the worst again, Dad." Nicole stood up, too, and began clearing the table. "Don't you have any faith in Jane's judgment? She's never done anything foolhardy in her life."

"She's never had that much money in her life, either. When I suggested that Breck should sign a prenuptial agreement, she became indignant."

"I can understand her reaction," Nicole said. "You were inferring that the man she loved couldn't be trusted."

"Well, *can* he be? What if he's a gigolo? And what about that Chase character? What if he uses treasure hunting as some sort of flimflam?"

"This conversation has come full circle," Nicole said, carrying the plates into the kitchen.

Her father followed her. "What we need is more information. Why don't you see what you can dig up?"

Nicole shook her head. "No, that wouldn't be right. Toby is Jane's husband now, and I don't think she would appreciate me snooping into his background."

"Then look into Chase's background."

"I'm not a private investigator, Dad. I wouldn't even know where to start."

"Use your research training," her father suggested.

"All right," she agreed reluctantly. "I'll see what I can find out about his sunken treasure venture, anyway."

"Good girl." Her father patted her back.

Nicole knew that he wanted her to handle the situation and leave him out of it. She'd accepted her father's distance from family matters at a very early age. She believed he was sincerely worried about his sister, but she also knew that his work consumed most of his time and energy.

"Don't worry, Dad," she said. "I'll watch over Jane."

"I knew I could count on you, my dear." He patted her back again.

Nicole took off her reading glasses and rubbed her tired eyes. She'd spent five fruitless hours at the Boston public library perusing microfilmed newspaper and magazine articles about treasure hunters. Not one of them had mentioned Gregory Chase. She'd cross-referenced so much that she was sure her eyes were getting crossed. She gazed up at the high ceiling for a moment to rest them, then perched her horn-rimmed glasses back on her nose and continued reading the magazine article on the screen. It had been written by a wealthy widow named Susan Fitzwell, who had invested in underwater salvage expeditions around the world. Nicole found Mrs. Fitzwell's gushy, self-serving style irritating but patiently persevered. A moment later the name Greg Chase jumped off the screen and hit her square between her weary eyes. As Nicole continued to read, all her worst fears were confirmed.

"There's no denying that Greg Chase has oodles of charm," Mrs. Fitzwell reported. She went on to describe his physical charms in detail. Already well aware of them, Nicole skimmed over that part. "He completely bamboozled me, I admit," Mrs. Fitzwell continued. "He took my money and gave me nothing in return. Mr. Chase's modus operandi is to ensnare innocent tourists who stay at his inn, the Sea Rover, with his romantic tales about sunken treasure. He claims that he's searching for a seventeenth-century wreck named the Buenaventura, but I've since learned from highly reliable sources that no galleon of that period ever sank in the vicinity of Saint Sophia. I have no idea how many poor souls like me Mr. Chase has hoodwinked, but I dare say they number in the hundreds."

Mrs. Fitzwell went on to discuss a more successful venture in the Florida Keys. Nicole stopped reading. She had found what she'd been looking for but felt no joy in the accomplishment.

She left the library and walked back to her apartment on Commonwealth Avenue, ten blocks away. Clutching the fur collar of her burgundy wool coat to her neck, she lowered her head against the cold, merciless blast of the January wind. Although the sidewalks were icy and she had to navigate dirty mounds of snow at each street crossing, Nicole walked at a brisk pace and would have run if the going hadn't been so treacherous. Once inside her brownstone building, she hurried up the three flights of stairs to her apartment, shucked her coat, then went straight to the telephone. She dialed the operator and asked how to put through a call to Saint Sophia.

It took awhile for the connection to go through and during that time Nicole found herself hoping that Greg Chase wouldn't answer. At the same time, she felt a strange excitement at the likelihood that he would and tensed in preparation.

"Hello, the Sea Rover speaking here. How may I help you, if you don't mind?" a woman with a lilting accent answered.

The accent, the phrasing and the unexpected voice confused Nicole for a moment. "I'd like to speak with Ms. Webster, please."

"Let me apologize for your wrong number, dear lady," came the response.

"Are you sure Jane Webster isn't staying there?"

"Oh, you are inquiring for Madame *Breck*! But of course she is here. Such misadventures she has suffered lately!"

"What? Is my aunt all right?"

"Your auntie? Ah! You must then be Nicole Niece who lives in the state of Boston. What a pretty picture you are, which your auntie showed me. Come to Saint Sophia, who don't you, and let me fatten you up with my mango pie. I make the best on the island."

"Is my aunt all right?" Nicole asked again.

"More fit than any violin you'd want to play," came the singsong assurance. "That monster Soufrière hurt her ankle but it is mending nicely. And not a harmed hair from the car mishappening, thank the Lord. Your auntie almost drove off the mountain, and what a long tumble that would have been for Madame Breck. All the way down to the sea below!''

Nicole gasped. ''Aunt Jane had a car accident?''

''Should I not have mentioned it to you, perhaps? Greg Mister tells me all the time I chatter too much about which is best left unspoken. Here he is now, standing at my shoulder, making that glaring look. You speak to *him*, Nicole Niece.''

''No!'' she cried. ''I want to speak to Ja—''

''How are you, Nickie?'' a deep voice interrupted.

Nicole steeled herself. ''Never mind how I am, Chase. I want to know how Jane is.''

''Don't worry. She's perfectly fine,'' he calmly replied. ''That was the housekeeper, Marie, you were talking to. She tends to exaggerate. Not intentionally. She just has a unique way of expressing herself. She can speak a little French and Spanish, and she's fluent in the island patois, of course, but English remains a slightly garbled mystery to her.''

Nicole refused to be sidetracked by a discussion of Marie's language skills. Or by Chase's easy manner, either. How could she believe anything *he* said? ''Could you get Jane for me, please?''

''She's out with Toby at the moment. He carried her down to the beach to enjoy the sunset.''

''He carried her?''

''Because of her ankle. The doctor assured us it's only a strain, but Toby insists on pampering her.''

''How did she get this sprained ankle?''

''Strained,'' he corrected.

Nicole could feel the patience draining out of her at a dangerous rate. She gripped the telephone harder.

"Marie said some kind of monster called a *soufrière* hurt her."

His husky chuckle came over the long-distance line. "Soufrière is the name of the volcano on this island, Nickie. In fact, most volcanoes throughout the Caribbean are called that. Don't ask me why."

"I won't. All I want to know is what happened to Jane."

"Toby took her to see Soufrière. While they were exploring she lost her footing and twisted her ankle."

Nicole imagined her aunt almost falling into a deep, steamy caldron, never to be seen again. "Why did Toby take her to such a dangerous place?" she demanded.

"Soufrière hasn't been active for decades," Greg replied.

"What about the car accident? Your housekeeper said that Jane almost drove off the side of the mountain."

"It wasn't as dramatic as that. Jane took the Jeep to town and a tire blew out on the way. She lost control for a moment but managed to stop in plenty of time. Trust me, Nickie, you needn't be concerned."

Trust him? Was he joking? "Please have Jane call me as soon as she returns."

"Will do." His voice became less breezy, more intimate. "I've been thinking a lot about you since the wedding, Nickie."

"Really?" she asked with cold disbelief.

"I'm sorry I couldn't make that dinner with you and your father, but something important came up. You got my message, I hope."

"Yes." She considered mentioning that she got his hotel bill, too, but decided against it. She didn't bring up Mrs. Fitzwell's article, either. If Chase knew that she was on to him, he wouldn't be inclined to relay her message to Jane. The less said to him the better, Nicole decided. "Well, goodbye, Chase. Don't forget to tell Jane to get back to me." Her hand was trembling when she replaced the receiver. What enraged her most was that he'd had the gall to ask her to trust him!

As she waited for Jane's call, Nicole tried not to think the worst. But that proved impossible. She could not get it out of her mind that Jane had been married for less than a week and had already met with two accidents. If she had a fatal one, Breck would be left a wealthy widower. Attempting to shake off such horrible suspicions, Nicole paced in front of the telephone. She was being ridiculous, she told herself. Or was she? She stopped pacing. What kind of protection did Jane have on an isolated Caribbean island? Were there police in Saint Sophia to investigate whether a woman had fallen into a volcano or been pushed? Or if a tire had been tampered with?

When Jane returned her call an hour later, relief flooded through Nicole. She pressed her aunt for details about her mishaps. Jane laughed off the incidents and sounded so blissfully happy that Nicole couldn't bring herself to tell her what she'd discovered about Greg Chase. Besides, she had no evidence that Toby Breck was involved in Chase's sunken treasure scam.

"I received your letter this morning," Jane said. "I wish you hadn't gone on and on thanking me for the house, dear. It made perfect sense for me to give it to you, since I have no use for it anymore."

"But it was such a generous gift, Jane! I'm going to spend some time there working on my next book before I go on another lecture tour."

"I have a much better idea. Why don't you come to Saint Sophia instead? You could stay in one of the cottages and have all the peace and quiet you need to work."

"All right," Nicole said without the slightest hesitation. "I'll fly down tomorrow."

"What? You really will? Frankly, I'm stunned that you finally accepted my invitation."

Nicole was just as surprised by her spontaneous decision. She rarely did anything spontaneously. But she felt a compelling need to see her aunt, to make sure all was really well with her.

"What made you change your mind?" Jane asked.

"Oh, slogging through snowdrifts as I walked back from the library today, I suppose," Nicole answered, again fighting back the temptation to tell Jane what she'd discovered there. It would be much better to tell her in person. Even better to confront Chase with it first and hear his side of the story. Yes, that would be the best way to handle it.

"You can't take a direct flight to Saint Sophia," Jane told her. "There's no airport. You'll have to land in Saint Lucia and then take a seaplane here. Tell me as soon as you know what time you'll be arriving. I'll meet you at the dock. Oh, I'm so thrilled you're coming, dear! Sleep well. I'll see you tomorrow."

Nicole didn't sleep well at all, though. She dreamed that she was captain of a galleon, and a pirate attacked it. They engaged in a strenuous sword fight, a fight she felt sure she could win. But then he made a few quick, fancy maneuvers and thrust his blade right into her heart! Nicole's eyes flew open. She pressed her palm to her breast and could feel her heart pounding. Only a silly nightmare, she thought with great relief. Still, she tossed and turned for the rest of the night.

When she boarded a plane to the Caribbean the next morning, the nightmare still troubled her. She couldn't shake off the memory of looking straight into the pirate's green eyes as his sword plunged into her heart and *smiling* at him. That was the most troubling part of her dream. Why had she smiled?

Chapter Four

Greg waited on the rickety pier, frowning as he gazed up at the clear azure sky. The impending arrival of Jane's niece disturbed him. Why had she suddenly decided to come to Saint Sophia? He doubted it was for some fun in the sun. Nicole Webster probably had an exceptionally large vocabulary, but Greg doubted that the word fun was in it. After reading her book, his initial opinion of her had been confirmed. The proper Ms. Webster was a patronizing, humorless pedant. That she'd practically hung up on him when she'd called yesterday hadn't tempered his opinion of her, either.

Still, Greg couldn't deny that he found her physically attractive, and that irritated him even more. He wished he hadn't told her that he'd been thinking about her. Her reaction to his confession had been less than heartwarming. He couldn't get his last image of her out of his mind, though. She'd looked so damn lovely in that thin ruffled gown as the snow swirled around her—so fair and slender and vulnerable. Vulnerable? Greg shook his head. Ice queens were invincible.

He glimpsed a spot on the horizon. The small seaplane bringing Nicole to Saint Sophia was coming in. And Greg felt a hum of anticipation run through him, despite his reservations about the lady.

Nicole pressed her forehead against the cabin window, enchanted by her first view of Saint Sophia. She hadn't expected the island to look so lush and verdant. A golden beach rimmed it, and a spine of mountains ran the length of it. It looked like some magical place where anything was possible. She felt a pleasant little flutter of anticipation.

Then the little plane dipped and her stomach lurched. Pleasure receded and fear took over. During her twenty-minute flight from the neighboring island, Nicole had come to the conclusion that the pilot was a madman. He'd sung dirty ditties at the top of his lungs the whole time, and now he was shouting "Geronimo!" as the plane dived straight into the glittering turquoise sea below.

This is it, the end of my short, rather uneventful life, Nicole thought grimly, regretting that it had been so uneventful. She wished that she had taken more chances when she'd had the opportunity, instead of being so circumspect. She wished that she had been more spontaneous, less guarded. Her experience had been so limited. And now she was going to...

No, she wasn't going to die, after all, Nicole realized, as the plane's pontoons bounced on the water and some of it splashed through a crack in the door and onto her taupe linen skirt.

After a brief sigh of relief, Nicole forgot all about her frantic last regrets and wishes. As the plane glided toward the pier, the sight of Gregory Chase captured her attention completely.

He stood with his hands in the pockets of white cotton trousers, the breeze ruffling his dark, thick hair. The sleeves of his loose-fitting muslin shirt were rolled up, showing off his tanned, muscular forearms. The shirt was collarless and the front placket unbuttoned. It occurred to Nicole that it was the sort of shirt a buccaneer would wear. She shivered, remembering her dream, and placed her hand against her chest, as if shielding her heart.

The pilot opened the cabin door and gave her a boost out. Greg leaned over the edge of the pier and offered her his hand. She took it, feeling the strength of his grasp as he hoisted her up. For an instant Nicole was dazzled by his green eyes and almost lost her balance.

"Welcome to Saint Sophia," he said, giving her a brief kiss on the cheek, so brief that it could have been the soft, warm breeze against her skin.

He needed a haircut, she noticed. And a shave. He'd been perfectly groomed at the wedding, but now a few days' growth of beard shadowed his strong jaw. Nicole found this both annoying and oddly exciting.

"I expected Jane to meet me," she said.

"I volunteered."

"How kind of you."

He shrugged. "I needed to pick up some supplies in town, so I figured I might as well pick you up, too. Kill two birds with one stone."

"How graciously put, Chase." He'd managed to put her on the defensive less than two minutes after she'd arrived, Nicole noted. She tugged at her hand, which he still grasped in his big palm.

Greg grinned and released it. "You're looking good, Nickie."

Lord, so he! she thought. "Have you decided to grow a beard?" she asked.

"Actually, I'm growing it back," he replied, rubbing his chin. "Shaved it off for Jane's wedding."

"Personally, I don't much care for beards."

His grin expanded. "Personally, I don't care much if you don't."

"Of course not. I'm sorry I mentioned it," Nicole quickly apologized. Why had she? What Chase chose to do with that smug face of his was none of her business.

"Here's your suitcase, lady," the pilot called.

He threw it onto the pier and it skittered across a few splintered planks. Nicole winced, sure that the leather had been scarred. He gave a jaunty wave, climbed back into the cockpit and buzzed off.

"That pilot flies like a lunatic daredevil," Nicole said as soon as the sound of the plane's engine had receded and conversation was possible again. "I was sure we were going to crash-land."

"He's never lost a passenger yet," Greg assured her. "You've got to go with the flow when you're down here. Relax and take things in stride."

"Easier said than done when your very life is in danger!" She frowned, remembering what had motivated her to come to Saint Sophia. "I can't wait to see Jane. Is the Sea Rover far from here?"

"About an hour's drive."

"That long? But the island's so small."

"But the roads are very winding. We have to go through the mountains to get to the other side of the island." He picked up her suitcase. "Hey, what did you pack this with? Rocks?"

"Books."

He laughed. "Figures. You don't intend to spend your whole time here with your pretty nose stuck in a book, do you, Nickie?"

He lightly tapped the tip of it, and Nicole couldn't help but smile at his teasing. "No one calls me Nickie, Chase."

"I do. But I won't if you don't like it."

"No, I don't mind." In truth, she liked the way the nickname sounded when he drawled it out. She liked it more than she should.

"Well, I mind you calling me Chase," he said. "I wish you'd stop doing that. You make it sound as if I'm your adversary."

Was he? Perhaps. But Nicole had resolved to give him the benefit of the doubt until she knew for sure. "I didn't mean to give that impression, Greg," she said.

"Much better." He squeezed her arm.

Every time he touched her, Nicole's heart rate increased. An overreaction, she knew, but one she couldn't help. Despite his seemingly easygoing nature, Greg made her terribly nervous. "I hope this isn't an imposition for you. My staying at the Sea Rover, I mean. If it is I'll find another—"

"Don't be silly!" he interrupted. "There's plenty of room. Hell, there's *always* plenty of room." He shifted her suitcase to his other hand. "Come on. My chariot awaits. You'll enjoy the ride."

More than the plane ride, Nicole hoped. She walked beside Greg down the pier, and as they approached a group of rough-looking fishermen in tattered clothing, she automatically reached for his arm. But they proved to be a friendly lot, smiling and tipping their tricornered black felt hats to Nicole. Greg greeted most of them by name and spoke with them in a dialect she couldn't understand.

"The men who make their living fishing off this island are a freewheeling bunch," Greg told Nicole after they'd left the pier. "I admire their independence. They dress that way deliberately, you know. The more ragtag they look, the better. It's part of their style. The felt hats go back for centuries. And so do their dugout canoes." He pointed to a beached one. "Notice the bow. The design comes from the rams of Carib war canoes."

Nicole found this fascinating. "I'd like to research Carib legends and history while I'm here."

"A busman's holiday, huh? You know what they say about all work and no play, Nickie."

"Are you implying that I'm dull?" She released her hold on his arm and instantly missed the solid touch of the hard flesh beneath his thin muslin shirt.

"I read your book," he said instead of answering her question.

That surprised her. And her expression must have showed it because Greg chuckled. "Didn't you think I could read, Nickie?"

"I didn't think you'd be interested."

"I was more than interested, I was highly amused."

"I intended to be informative, not amusing, when I wrote *Courtship Rituals*," Nicole stated in her precise, clipped voice. "And I doubt you really read it."

He cleared his throat. "Romance is a cultural development that contrives to put our basic sexual needs on an artificial level, resulting in modern-day confusion and disappointment."

It was an exact quote from her book and her surprise turned to amazement. "That's right!"

"No, it's hogwash," he muttered.

"Hogwash!" she sputtered.

He stopped suddenly, dropped her suitcase, and placed his large, tanned hands on her slender shoulders. Nicole stiffened, sure that he was about to kiss her, yet not sure what her response was going to be. But he didn't attempt to kiss her.

"Take a deep breath and smell the flowers, Nickie," he commanded. "Let the warm, moist, tropical air fill your lungs. You've traveled over two thousand miles to get here, but you haven't taken a moment to appreciate the sublime beauty surrounding you." He shook his head as he stared down at her. "You might as well still be in frigid Boston, lady."

She shrugged off his hands. But she did take a deep breath, inhaling sweet scents, and she did look around, taking in the sparkling bay, the grove of coconut palms fringing the golden strand of beach, the rolling hillsides beyond. "Lovely," she pronounced perfunctorily. "Now can we please get going?"

Greg sighed. "You'll fall under the romantic spell of Saint Sophia eventually, Nickie."

He picked up her suitcase again and led the way up the beach toward the palm grove, where he'd parked his open Jeep in the shade. Nicole followed him, getting sand in her open-toed espadrilles. She didn't want to fall under any spell while she was here. She wanted to keep a clear head.

The ride to his inn turned out to be one of the bumpiest Nicole had ever experienced. The rutted, mostly unpaved road twisted up the range of mountains bisecting the island, then dipped deep into valleys. At times the road dangerously skirted the mountainside. And Greg was driving on the left, which made her feel even more uncomfortable.

Before he took each of the many sharp turns, he always tooted his horn three times. "Why do you do that?" Nicole asked after the second hairpin maneuver.

"In case someone's coming in the opposite direction. Everyone who owns a motor vehicle on the island has a code toot. So you always know who's coming around the bend before you see them."

Before you crash right into them, Nicole thought. "Is this the road where Jane had her accident?"

"Yep. It's the only road there is. But it wasn't really an accident. It was a flat tire. Happens all the time."

"Then I don't think it's safe for my aunt to drive alone. I'm surprised Toby let her."

"He's her husband, not her keeper."

Nicole certainly wasn't going to dispute that. As Greg tooted again and negotiated another swerve, she held her breath. She released it with a deep sigh of relief once he'd succeeded. "This is worse than a roller coaster," she said.

"You get accustomed to it after a few trips. It's not as treacherous as it appears."

Nicole looked down at the sea hundreds of feet below and gave an involuntary shudder. "Then appearances can certainly be deceiving."

"That's right, Nickie. They can be. You should keep that in mind while you're here." His smile was totally disarming. "And stop clenching your fists. You're perfectly safe. Why don't you sit back, relax and enjoy the scenery?"

Nicole did relax after a while, satisfied that Greg was a competent, careful driver. The twisting route they took meandered through a cool mini-rain forest where delicate tree ferns lined the road, past modest wooden huts with luxurious gardens of tropical flowers, through a sleepy little village where pigs and chickens wandered as freely as the children. Orange blossoms scented the air.

"Agriculture is the basis of the island's economy," Greg told her as they passed a plantation.

"Those are banana trees, aren't they?"

"Banana plants," he corrected. "The trunks are really layers of leaves wrapped around each other. The root is a rhizome. It's one of the fruits mentioned in the earliest Sanskrit writings."

She looked at him, impressed that he knew that. *She* hadn't.

"The Spanish brought the banana to Saint Sophia from the Canary Islands," he continued. "They also brought slaves from Africa to man the plantations. A majority of Sophians are of African descent."

He went on to give her a history of the island, beginning with its discovery by Christopher Columbus. Nicole leaned back and listened, mesmerized both by his detailed knowledge and his soothing voice, as he talked about the European colonization of the island, the constant warring between the Spanish and the French to take control of Saint Sophia for centuries, and its own fight for independence during the present one.

"You sound more like a teacher than a treasure hunter," she couldn't help commenting.

"That's because I used to be a history professor," he said. "My specialty was Spanish colonialism, starting with Cortés and his gang of conquistadors."

"Is that right?" Nicole more easily pictured him as a conquistador than a professor, though. "What made you give up the profession?"

"My quest," Greg replied succinctly.

He'd captivated her completely now. "Your *quest*? You mean like for the Holy Grail or something?" Was he teasing her again? she wondered.

"Yeah, something like that." There was a distant sound of a horn. Two toots and then four. Greg came to a full stop and pressed his own horn three times. "Brace yourself, Nickie. That was Soufrière's warning signal."

"I thought Soufrière was a volcano."

"Also the islanders' nickname for their one public transportation vehicle. You'll understand why in a minute."

And then she saw it coming around the bend like a bat out of hell. No—more like a raging, roaring dragon charging straight at them, spewing the black smoke of doom. In fact, it was only a rattling old bus that needed a new muffler, but Nicole was sure it was traveling at least sixty miles an hour. "There isn't room for both of us on this road!" she cried out, sure that the only way Greg could possibly get out of the way was by driving off the mountain itself.

"Plenty of room," he assured her calmly.

There was a tooth-aching screech of brakes and the bus slowed down to a snail's pace. It crawled by the Jeep with only inches between them, and the passengers waved and called out gaily from the open windows. They spoke the same language as the fishermen, and Greg addressed many of them by name, too.

"Who be the pretty miss?" an old woman asked him in English. Her skin was the color of yellowed parchment and her amber eyes slanted. She smiled at Nicole, showing gaps between her teeth. "Relation of the Bird Lady, I venture from the look of her."

"Her niece," Greg told the old woman.

"You come visit me sometime soon, Niece," she commanded Nicole. "I'll tell you the future for very little charge. Greg Mister knows where I live."

The bus passed by, picked up speed and careened down the road. Nicole turned to watch it disappear, leaving a cloud of fumes in its wake.

"Who was that strange woman?" she asked Greg.

"Anabella Roseau. She's a witch."

Nicole's eyes widened. "How marvelous! She looked more Asian than African."

"She's a Carib Indian. There aren't too many of them left on this island."

"I definitely want to visit her," Nicole said.

"So she can tell you the future? I'm surprised a pragmatic soul like you believes in soothsayers."

"I don't. It's the past I want her to tell me about. Perhaps she knows some interesting Indian legends."

"She does. They've all been passed down to her." He put the Jeep into gear. "Along with her acknowledged magical powers."

Nicole smiled at that. "Do you believe in magic, Greg?"

"Deep down everyone does."

"Not me!"

"You will before you leave Saint Sophia, Nickie."

She gave him a sidelong glance. His tone had been light, not menacing at all, yet for some reason she construed his blithe statement as a personal threat.

A short while later he turned off the mountain road and took an even bumpier, narrower side track, lined with dense, flowering hedges. The brilliant violet blossoms tempted Nicole, and she reached out to pluck one!

"Careful!" Greg warned.

But it was too late. Nicole let out a cry of pain and pulled back her hand. The tip of her index finger was bleeding.

Greg stopped the car. "The stems of bougainvillea have very sharp thorns," he said, taking her injured hand in his. He examined it closely. "Just a prick. Luckily the thorn didn't get imbedded." He produced a linen handkerchief from his back pocket and pressed it against her finger. "It'll stop bleeding in a minute."

He continued to hold her hand, and Nicole slowly raised her eyes to meet his. That was more of a mistake than reaching for the flower, she realized, again too late. She became lost in his shimmering green gaze and felt powerless to prevent their lips from meeting, too. His wide mouth covered hers, softly, gently, and her own opened like the lush blossom she'd tried to capture. But now it was she who was captured, utterly, by his deepening kiss. The taste of him excited her more than she'd imagined possible. Her mind told her to push him away, right now, this very instant, but her body refused to comply.

He was the one who eventually broke their long, lingering kiss. He tilted his head to look at her, a bemused smile on his lips. "That was even better than I expected."

So he'd expected it, had he? Well, she hadn't. She couldn't believe that she'd reacted so strongly. So stupidly. And even as she chastised herself, a part of her longed to have him kiss her again. "Your beard scratches," she muttered.

He laughed. "I knew you'd find something to criticize." He took away the handkerchief. "There, it's stopped bleeding." He released her hand. "No harm done."

Without another word he drove on. At a loss for words herself, Nicole kept her face averted and the treacherous, gorgeous bougainvillea became a violet blur as she stared out at the hedges lining the road. No harm done, she kept repeating to herself. No harm done.

The road turned out to be a long driveway leading to a large, brick two-story house with a wide veranda and louvered windows. On a rise to take advantage of the sea breezes, the house was surrounded by sloping emerald lawns decorated with gaudy, tangled beds of lilies, poinsettia, hibiscus and frangipani. It would have taken Nicole's breath away if Greg's kiss hadn't done that already.

"So this is the Sea Rover," she said, barely managing to find her voice again. "It's so . . . grand."

"One of the last original plantation houses left on the island," Greg said. "Built out of ballast, brick joined with molasses-and-sand cement in the eighteenth century. But it's more rundown than grand. That charming red tile roof leaks, the plumbing is archaic, and when the generator breaks down, which is often, we have to make do with kerosene lamps or candles. Needless to say, there's no air-conditioning. Just ceiling fans. And don't expect hot water. Or cold, for that matter. Tepid is all you get."

"Who could ask for more?" Nicole asked, relieved that they had the house to talk about now, relieved that Greg was acting as if nothing had happened between them a few moments ago. As far as Nicole was concerned, that foolish incident was best forgotten and she intended to do just that.

She saw Jane then, coming across the lawn arm in arm with Toby Breck. Nicole still couldn't get used to the fact that this toothy, towheaded man was now her aunt's husband. Barefoot, dressed in boldly patterned shorts and a yellow T-shirt, he looked more like a boy of thirteen than a man of thirty. But her aunt looked like a teenager, too, Nicole noticed as she came closer. Jane's hair was in a swinging braid, her cheeks and nose were sunburned, and she was wearing a sundress in bright awning stripes of red and gold. Her smile was as wide and as guileless as Toby's.

Nicole climbed out of the Jeep and ran to her. They embraced with the enthusiasm of long-lost relatives, although it had only been a week since they'd seen each other.

"I can't believe you're really here!" Jane said.

"How *are* you?" Nicole asked a bit too intensely.

"Why, I'm fine, dear. Why shouldn't I be?"

"Well, your ankle."

Jane laughed. "But that was nothing. I'm not even limping anymore. I've never felt better in my life."

"That's good. You really do look wonderful, Jane."

"Marriage agrees with me."

If appearances could be trusted, that seemed to be true. Jane positively glowed. Nicole turned to Toby and offered her hand. "I bet you didn't expect to see me again so soon."

"I'm glad you came, Nicole," he said and sounded sincere.

"Yes, we're all one big happy family now," Jane chirped. "I wish you could stay forever, dear."

With his long, easy gait, Greg approached them carrying Nicole's suitcase. "How long *do* you plan to stay?" he asked her.

Pushing the memory of his kiss to the very back of her mind, Nicole dared to look at him directly again.

His face was expressionless. "Well, that depends," she replied.

"Depends on what?"

On how long it takes me to be satisfied that Jane is safe and happy, she silently answered. "On how long it takes me to wear out my welcome," she said aloud.

"That could never happen, dear," Jane assured her. "You should stay until you have to go on your next lecture tour. As I mentioned during our phone conversation yesterday, you can have a private cottage all to yourself to work undisturbed. Unless you'd prefer to be in the main house with us."

"Let me show Nickie the cottage first," Greg said, taking her arm. "If she doesn't like it, she can have a room at the house, of course."

But from the way he was tugging at her arm now, he was giving Nicole the distinct impression that he wanted her to settle in at the cottage, not the house. He led her across the lawn and down a sandy path edged with tropical flora. She could see the glistening sea about fifty yards beyond. Ahead, three whitewashed stone buildings, spaced a good distance apart for privacy, were nestled in the luxuriant foliage. Each one had a shady little porch and a thick thatched roof.

"I'm beginning to believe that I really have landed in paradise," she said as she followed him to the first cottage.

"Don't forget the thorns in the bougainvillea," Greg reminded her.

Why had he brought that up now? Nicole wondered. Was it a subtle warning? She remained as wary as ever of him although a part of her longed to trust him completely. But her intellect, impervious to a man's persuasive touch and lips, cautioned her how irrational that would be. How reckless.

"No, Nickie, Saint Sophia isn't paradise by a long shot," Greg went on. "For the last fifty years or so it's been relatively peaceful here, but the economy fluctuates and there's a degree of poverty. I'd like to see this island become self-sufficient one day and not turn into just another tourist spot."

His concern sounded sincere. "Do you intend to make Saint Sophia your home for good?" she asked him.

He laughed. "I never intended to stay as long as I have! I live day to day, Nickie, and never give much thought to the future. The only goals I concentrate on are my immediate ones."

"Which are?"

He threw open the cottage door without replying, and Nicole stepped into a large, airy room with stucco walls painted shell pink. The bleached pinewood floors were decorated with puddles of golden sunlight and a scattering of sisal rugs. A breeze wafted through the windows, and the old-fashioned ceiling fan made slow, lazy circles above a four-poster bed swathed in gauzy netting.

"The netting is just for effect," Greg told her. "Thanks to the World Health Organization, mosquitoes aren't a problem on the island. But it adds a romantic touch, don't you think?" He laughed. "I forgot. You don't put much stock in romance, do you?"

She turned her eyes from the beautiful, inviting bed to look him full in the face. What she saw was a man too handsome for his own good. Or hers. "No, Chase, I don't."

"The offer I made in Vermont is still good, sweetheart. I'll be happy to teach you the value of romance."

She had no intention of playing coy games with this man. "You'd be wasting your time. That kiss was a big mistake, Chase. And it's not going to happen again."

His smile demonstrated disbelief. He took her hand and lifted it to his cheek, rubbing her soft palm against his rough bristles. "Not even if I shave?"

"Don't bother," she replied, pulling back her hand.

"No bother. I've decided to make you my immediate goal, Nickie. You think you're up to the challenge?"

So he wanted a challenge, did he? Nicole crossed her hands over her chest. "You owe me two hundred sixty-eight dollars and forty-two cents, mister," she said. She'd decided the time had come to have it out with him.

Chapter Five

Greg looked amused. "That's a very precise figure." His eyes slowly roamed over hers. "How did you come up with it, Nickie?"

"It's the amount I paid the proprietor of the Bear and Elk to cover for you and Toby last week," Nicole replied coldly. "What shoddy behavior, Chase! And to think that you're an innkeeper yourself. How would you like it if your guests ran out without paying their bill?"

"You're certainly eager to assume the worst about me," he replied, no longer amused.

"What else can I assume?"

"You could have asked me for an explanation rather than accuse me of being a welsher."

Nicole almost laughed at his injured tone, but seeing the sparks of anger in his eyes, she thought better of it. "Yes, an explanation is surely in order," she said.

Her holier-than-thou attitude didn't make Greg inclined to give her one, though. He didn't have to answer to her. Or anyone. In Saint Sophia he was his own man, as freewheeling as the fishermen on the pier. What did he owe Nicole Webster? He sighed. As far as she reckoned, he owed her two hundred and sixty-eight dollars and forty-two cents.

"I intended to leave a check in the room," he said. "But I was in such a hurry to make the last flight back here that it slipped my mind."

"It slipped your mind," Nicole repeated sarcastically. "How convenient. Well, here I am to remind you about it." She held out her hand, palm up. "And to collect what you owe me."

Greg shrugged. "Sorry, lady. You'll have to go back to Vermont to collect. I already sent a check to Dickens at the inn. He seemed like an honest guy to me, so I'm sure he'll reimburse you when he receives it."

"Hah! *If* he receives it. Something tells me that checks from Gregory Chase tend to get lost in the mail."

"Watch it, Nickie," he warned. "As attractive as I find you, I may end up disliking you if you keeping making cracks like that."

"That's fine with me, Chase, because I don't want you to be attracted to me. Let's get that straight right now."

"Let's get another thing straight while we're at it. Tell me why you came to Saint Sophia," he demanded. "Surely not to collect on a bad debt, since the airfare here cost a lot more. There must have been a more compelling reason.''

"I came to see Jane, of course."

He smiled tightly. "I didn't think you came to see me, sweetheart. But why did you have such a sudden compulsion to visit your aunt?"

Although Greg hadn't made a move toward her, Nicole backed away from him, slamming her calves against the side of the bed. "I wanted to make sure she was all right."

"Why shouldn't Jane be all right?" He took a few steps closer.

Although the room was large, Nicole felt it to be a small, confining space at that moment. Chase was a man who made his presence felt in every corner. She brushed past him and went out to the porch, where she rested her hands on the rough railing and looked toward the sea.

Greg followed her out. "Why did you come here, Nickie?" he demanded again, his voice low and quiet behind her.

She took a deep breath. She disliked confrontations, but this one was necessary. "I know all about you, Chase. I guess I really came to tell you that. I want you to know that I'm on to you." She took another deep breath. "So you'd better watch your step."

She heard his soft chuckle. "Watch my step, sweetheart? That's pretty tough talk. What do you plan to do? Trip me up?" She felt the firm grip of his big hands on her shoulders and adrenaline shot through her.

She twisted away and turned to face him head-on. "You bet I do! You may have gotten away with swindling other rich women, but you're not going to do that to Jane. I'm not going to let you take advantage of her.''

There! It was out. She stiffened and waited for his reaction, closely observing his face. But it was a smooth tan mask that gave away nothing. Nothing at all. She'd expected a little more reaction than that.

"What the heck are you babbling about?" he finally asked her coolly.

Babbling, was she? Luckily she'd done her research. ''Does the name Susan Fitzwell ring a bell, Chase?''

Apparently it did. His eyes narrowed. "Yes, I know her," he replied.

"I discovered an article she wrote in a travel magazine. You were mentioned in it."

He nodded and rubbed the back of his head. "In none too flattering terms, as I recall."

"Oh, so you read it." Nicole was a little disappointed. She'd brought a copy of the article with her and on the plane trip down she'd imagined pulling it out of her purse and shaking it in his face. She'd imagined reading it aloud and seeing him squirm. She'd imagined this confrontation scene to be much more dramatic than it was actually turning out to be.

Chase simply smiled. "Of course I read it. Suzie sent it to me, air express, the day it was published." He shrugged. "Hell hath no fury like a woman scorned."

"Are you telling me that Mrs. Fitzwell became vindictive because you rejected her?"

"Something like that."

"In other words, you led her on, got her to invest in your phony venture, and then dumped her."

His lean face, shadowed by the dark stubble of beard, remained impassive. "Those are your words, lady, not mine." He ambled down the porch steps and paused on the last one to turn back and look at her. "I'm beginning to wish you'd never come to Saint Sophia, Nicole."

"What are you going to do? Order me to leave?"

"Of course not. Any guest of Jane's is welcome here. We usually have drinks on the veranda before dinner. Put in an appearance whenever you're ready. And we'll both keep *up* appearances for your aunt's sake, okay?"

"Don't worry, Chase. I won't tell Jane what I know about you unless I have to."

"You don't know a damn thing about me, Nicole," he replied. He turned his broad back on her and walked away.

She almost called him back but thought better of it. They had nothing more to say to each other.

A short while later Greg entered the brick house by the back door, rubbing his freshly shaved cheek.

"What's cooking, Marie?" he asked the tall, middle-aged woman stirring a big pot on the stove.

She turned to give him a haughty look. The orange and purple bandanna wrapped around her head accented her strong, handsome African features. "What are you doing in my kitchen, Greg Mister?"

Marie Blanco had laid down the law when he'd bought the inn. If he wanted her to stay on as chef and housekeeper, he would have to give her complete control of the kitchen. He'd happily agreed to that condition, and they had an excellent working relationship.

He'd given up trying to make her stop adding the "mister" after his first name when he'd realized that it was the proper way Sophian women addressed all men other than family relations. These islanders had a protocol they held firm to.

"I came to tell you that we're having an extra person for dinner tonight," he said.

"And don't you think I'm not already knowing it?" Marie asked in her convoluted English. "Madame Breck related the expected visitation of her niece to me last night. Is she as pretty as her picture?"

"She's extremely pretty," Greg allowed. Was that what made it so difficult to dislike her? But it was more than Nicole's cool blond looks that attracted him. She'd enraged him a few moments ago, yet at the same time he'd appreciated that she'd been up-front with him. He also admired her devotion to her aunt.

Or was she more concerned about Jane's fortune than her welfare? This possibility cut through Greg's mind, sharp as a knife. As Jane's most likely heir, Nicole would stand to benefit the most if her aunt's marriage broke up. Had she come to Saint Sophia to make trouble between Toby and Jane?

"Such a sudden, deep frown, Greg Mister," Marie said, looking at him with concern. "Caused by a headache, I hope not?"

"A slight headache," he replied. "One I shouldn't have too much trouble getting rid of." He would watch Nicole closely tonight, as closely as he knew she'd be watching him. And if he sensed she was trying to drive a wedge between Toby and Jane, he'd make damn sure she was on the next plane leaving the island.

But when Greg strolled out to the veranda and saw Nicole walking across the lawn, he felt a keen pleasure despite his suspicions. The setting sun bathed her in rosy light and made her loose, silky hair shimmer. She'd changed into a filmy white peasant dress that floated around her knees and left her shoulders bare. The sight of those beautifully molded pale shoulders made him a lot less inclined to want her on the next plane out. As much as she irritated him, she excited him. In fact it seemed the *more* she irritated him, the more she excited him. He decided that it wouldn't hurt to let her hang around for a while. Life on Saint Sophia had become far too comfortable for him and perhaps a little bit boring.

"You look beautiful," he called.

Nicole gave Greg a wary look as she approached. She hadn't expected him to flatter her now that she'd made her position and her opinion of him clear. He looked perfectly at ease and agreeable, though, leaning against the porch column, pretending to be delighted with her appearance. What a dissembler he was!

"Are we alone?" she asked, joining him on the veranda.

He nodded. "Toby and Jane haven't come down yet."

"Then you needn't be nice to me, Chase. Save the act for an audience."

"But I enjoy being nice to you, lovely lady. Here, sit down where you can get the best view of the garden and sea."

He took her hand and led her to a rattan settee with plump calico cushions. It was as if their last conversation had never taken place, and they'd parted on the friendliest terms possible. She noticed that he'd shaved. Surely not to please *her*. The possibility that he had, though, pleased her more than it should have.

"Would you care for a drink?" he asked.

"Thank you, I'd love one," she replied, matching his politeness.

He lifted a glass pitcher filled with a peach-colored liquid. "Marie's punch," he said, filling a tall glass. "It's an old island concoction and she won't divulge all the ingredients. But I've managed to discover that it contains brewed hibiscus flowers, papaya nectar, grenadine and dark rum." He handed the glass to Nicole. "It goes down smooth, but beware." He flashed his bright, white teeth. "The rum can sneak up on you and pack quite a wallop. Maybe that's why it's called passion punch. Once it gets into your system it can be devastating."

"I appreciate the warning. But I know exactly how much my system can take." Nicole gave him a look as frosty as the pitcher, then took a cautious sip.

"No, you'd never get drunk on passion, would you, Nicole?"

She lifted her elegant shoulders. "I wouldn't care for the hangover that's sure to follow." She placed the drink on the driftwood table in front of her. "I believe in moderation at all times, Chase."

"Such a sensible woman!" Laughing, Greg sat down beside her and lightly placed his hand on the back of her neck.

His fingers were chilled from the glass and his touch made her shiver. She leaned away from it and reached for her drink again. "I've barely seen Jane since I arrived," she said. "What could be keeping her and Toby?"

Greg laughed again.

"You seem to find everything I say amusing for some reason."

"Oh, come on, Nickie! Surely even *you* can figure out what would keep two honeymooners from leaving their bedroom."

"Oh, is that where they are?" Nicole cleared her throat awkwardly.

"I moved out of the main house to give them privacy," Greg said. "That's why I hoped you would choose to stay at a cottage, too."

She arched a sleek eyebrow. "You're staying at one of the cottages?"

"The one right next to yours, sweetheart. So if you ever hear anything go bump in the night, just call out my name."

"How comforting." Her tone was dry.

"It doesn't matter that you don't trust me, you know." He leaned closer to her and his breath was warm on her shoulder. She could feel the heat emanating from him, smell his heady masculine scent. "You'll still call out my name when you need me, Nicole." His low, quiet voice vibrated through her.

She didn't reply because she had no reply. Her pulse quickened, though. She could feel it throbbing at the base of her neck. She tilted back her head and took a long, deep sip of her cool drink.

"Delicious, isn't it?" Greg asked, watching her closely. "Once you have a small taste of passion, you become thirsty for more."

Her profile was etched like the finest cameo, he thought. The slant of her cheekbones thrilled him beyond measure. The long sweep of her throat excited him, and he longed to place his mouth against her throbbing pulse. And he would. Eventually.

At that moment Greg resolved to seduce Nicole Webster, to break through her cool exterior and get to the core of her heat. He knew it existed. He had known from the moment he'd kissed her. And what made it all the more exciting to him was that she would fight against it happening. She would fight with all her logic and intelligence. He'd never been one to back away from a challenge.

Nicole could feel his eyes boring into her and sat as still as a statue, determined to give nothing of herself away. She explained the flare of arousal Greg generated in her as a simple hormonal reaction. Perfectly human and normal and ordinary. Mother Nature had instilled in her the urge to mate, and an exceptionally fine male example of her particular species was sitting inches away from her, tantalizing her with not-so-subtle innuendos.

But she was no slave to biology. Oh no, not she. She was civilized, educated, and far too smart to fall for this particular rogue. If she weren't quite so civilized, in fact, she would dump her tall glass of passion punch right onto Gregory Chase's lap.

Instead, she handed it to him. "I've had enough of this," she said and forced herself to stand up and walk to the edge of the veranda. The sea breeze felt soothing against her heated skin.

"What a fantastic view," she remarked, keeping her back to him.

"It's fantastic, all right," he agreed, taking in her gently sloping shoulders, the small span of her waist, the alluring flare of her hips. He could see the outline of her long legs through the thin cotton of her dress. He was crazy about that dress and could only imagine her looking better without it. She wore dainty little flat sandals to show off her elegant, narrow feet. Feet he'd once caressed, he recalled. And would again. He'd caress every inch of her. Soon.

"I can't understand why your charming inn isn't filled with guests," she said in that high, fluty, precisely modulated Boston voice of hers.

Greg got up and joined Nicole, standing so close to her that their arms grazed. He smiled to himself when she drew back quickly. So she felt it, too—that sharp jolt of electricity every time they touched.

"Saint Sophia is a well-kept secret," he replied. "The last time the inn was filled was when Jane and her Audubon group were here. But they were devoted bird-watchers, not your average tourists. Most people have never heard of this place."

"Maybe you should advertise."

"I like things just the way they are," he said, his tone becoming brusque.

"Yes, I suppose you would, Chase, since all it takes is a rich gullible woman now and then to keep you going." Nicole waited breathlessly to see if she would get a reaction from him this time, sensing the possible danger of goading him too far.

She immediately felt his long, strong fingers around the back of her neck, felt the pressure of them against her soft, vulnerable flesh. But it was a gentle pressure, more like a caress.

"Does it give you a kick to say nasty things to me, sweetheart?" His voice was gentle, too, with an amused lilt to it, as if he were talking to a naughty child.

And because of that, Nicole was the one who became angry. She shrugged off his hand. "I only know what I've read about you, Chase."

"Don't believe everything you read. Especially when the author happens to be Suzie Fitzwell. If you met her, you'd know what I mean."

"Since that doesn't seem to be a very likely possibility, why don't you tell me what you mean?"

He shrugged. "Why should I? You wouldn't believe me anyway. And I'm not going to get down to Suzie's level and start slinging mud."

"Aren't you the noble one!" Her lips curled in a sarcastic smile. "Maybe Toby will be more inclined to give me some answers. Or more importantly, give some to Jane."

Faster than she could blink, Greg wrapped his hand around her upper arm and this time his touch wasn't gentle. "You leave Toby out of this, dammit. He wasn't even here when Suzie and I got involved."

Nicole stiffened. "Let go of my arm, Chase. You're hurting me."

"No, I'm not." He increased the pressure of his grip slightly, but he was right. He wasn't hurting her. Yet. "I want you to listen to me very carefully, Nicole. I care about my cousin as much as you care about Jane. So don't you dare interfere with their marriage."

Flame burned in Nicole's cheeks. She would not tolerate being bullied. "And don't you dare threaten me," she told him, doing the best she could to keep the quaver of fear out of her voice.

But Greg heard it and immediately released her arm. This wasn't the way to handle the situation, he cautioned himself. He took a deep breath. "I would never threaten or hurt you, Nicole. That's not the way I operate."

"How *do* you operate, Chase? That's what I want to know."

She found out a moment later, when Jane and Toby strolled through the open French doors.

"So you two finally decided to join us," Greg said in his smooth, easy manner. "Nicole and I were just talking about an article she read about me."

"About you?" Jane tilted her head, interested. "How nice."

"Not really." Greg gave her a rueful, disarming look that Nicole was sure he'd practiced many times in front of a mirror. "It wasn't a very flattering piece, Jane. The woman who wrote it more or less accused me of being a fraud."

"More than less," Nicole put in.

Jane looked shock and leaned against Toby. "But how dreadful, Gregory! Why on earth would someone write something like that about you?"

"Exactly my question," Nicole said. But she already knew Chase had outmaneuvered her. What a clever devil he was.

"What's this all about?" Toby demanded. "I don't understand. Does it have anything to do with the Buenaventura, Greg?"

"Yes, I'm afraid so." Greg ran a hand through his hair. "It all happened *months before you came* to

Saint Sophia, Toby," he stressed. "I let myself get talked into taking on an investment partner to keep the venture going. Money was tight at the time. I explained the risks to Mrs. Fitzwell, of course, but she still insisted on backing me." He shook his head, as if baffled by the whole experience. "Anyway, when I kept coming up from dives empty-handed, she bailed out. We had unpleasant words in parting, I admit. I never expected the lady to turn on me and write vicious lies, though. That wasn't fair play. But I guess life isn't fair, is it?" His resigned expression was one of an enduring martyr.

"Sue her!" Jane suggested.

"Lawyers take money," Greg reminded her.

"Well, don't let that stop you, Gregory. I'd be happy to offer you—"

"Please, Jane, no." He held up a halting hand. "I would never take money from you." He glanced over Jane's shoulder and gave Nicole a small, cold smile.

"It's always best to ignore those kinds of stories, anyway," Toby put in.

Nicole broke her gaze from Greg's and turned to him. "You mean there have been others?"

"Well, no. I mean...I don't know." Toby stuck his hands into the pockets of his gaudy shorts and looked confused. Then he looked at Greg, raising his sun-bleached eyebrows like question marks.

"You mean unfounded accusations in general, don't you?" Greg supplied.

"Yeah, right. Life's too short to let people hassle you."

Jane smiled approvingly at her husband, as if he'd just uttered deep philosophical wisdom. "How true, honey! Life's far too short for that."

He wrapped his arm around her waist. "And it's meant to be enjoyed to its fullest, bunny."

Greg groaned. "I don't know if I can endure much more of this mushy honey-bunny stuff from you two." His wide grin belied his objection. He beamed it full blast on Nicole. "They've been carrying on like this from the moment they met," he told her. "Ain't love grand?"

Or blind, she thought. But she couldn't keep herself from smiling, too, when she looked at Jane and Toby. They were the picture of wedded bliss. And because the last thing Nicole wanted was to put a damper on Jane's happiness, she dropped the subject of Mrs. Fitzwell and her damaging article. By the time Marie came out to announce that dinner was ready, it had long been forgotten—by everyone but Nicole, that was.

Jane introduced Nicole to the housekeeper.

Marie addressed Nicole, shaking her turbaned head. "If you are not most exceedingly careful during your stay here, you will suffer for it."

That sounded rather ominous to Nicole. "Suffer?"

"Indeed! I have seen it happen to other young ladies who have come to Sea Rover. Did they open their ears when I tried to warn them? Ah, if only they had!"

Nicole tensed. "What happened to them?"

"They could not take it," Marie replied. "And some far less fair than you. Is that not correct, Greg Mister?"

"Oh, they were far less fair than Nicole," he agreed.

"What couldn't they take?" Nicole demanded.

"The sun," Marie told her. "They burned very badly."

"Yes, Nicole will have to be careful not to get burned while she's here," Greg, said, cupping her bare, creamy shoulder with his palm and giving it a gentle squeeze. "But she's careful by nature, so you needn't worry, Marie."

"Some young ladies forget to be careful when they come to Saint Sophia," Marie said.

"Oh, I won't," Nicole assured her.

They ate dinner on the open patio, under a canopy of stars and in the glow of candles that flickered in hurricane lamps. After ladling out the first course, a fragrant stew, Marie joined them and watched intently as Nicole brought the spoon to her lips.

"It's delicious," Nicole said. "What's in it?"

"Crapaud," Marie replied.

"And what's that?"

"Mountain chicken, dear," Jane said, then quickly changed the subject. "How was your flight to the island?"

"Don't ask!" Nicole said. "Is mountain chicken a type of fowl indigenous to the island?"

"Don't ask," Greg advised.

"Why, it's frog, Nicole Niece," Marie informed her. "Everybody knows that."

"Everybody but Nicole Niece," Greg drawled, catching her dismayed expression. That's what she got for asking too many questions. He winked at her. "Eat up, sweetheart."

He was surprised when she did just that, quickly overcoming her initial repulsion and finishing the stew with a great show of gusto.

Although she'd enjoyed the stew, Nicole was relieved that the main course was broiled langouste, the local lobster. Sweet and tender, it was served with buttered breadfruit, which had a texture a little softer than a baked potato and a tangy wine flavor that Nicole found delicious.

"That breadfruit was from a backyard tree," Marie told her. "As were the mangoes in my famously delicious pie that I made to honor your visitation to our island."

After they had Marie's famously delicious pie and a strong, rich coffee made from locally grown beans, Toby began to yawn.

"Pardon me," he said to Nicole. "But no matter how much coffee I drink, I still start getting sleepy around nine or so." He got up and stretched, then gave his bride a pointed look that didn't look the least bit sleepy to Nicole.

"You go to bed, honey," Jane told him. "I'll be up in a little while."

"When?" he asked, crestfallen.

"I haven't had a moment alone with Nicole since she's come, Tobias," Jane said, taking his hand and pressing it to her cheek. "We're going to stay up and talk awhile."

"But you know I can't go to sleep without my cuddle bunny," Toby told his bride.

This was getting downright embarrassing! Nicole thought. "We'll have plenty of time to talk tomorrow, Jane," she said. "It's been a long day and I think

I'll turn in myself." She stood up, nodded to Toby and Greg, bowed to Marie, and kissed her aunt.

"I'll walk you to your cottage, Nicole," Greg said.

And before she could object that it wasn't necessary, he was by her side and had a firm grip on her arm.

Their footsteps were silent as they crossed the thick, plush lawn in the dark. The only light came from the moon and Nicole was grateful that Greg had accompanied her.

"No streetlights," she said.

"We have the stars to guide us." He stopped and put his arm around her waist. "Look up, Nicole. Have you ever seen stars appear so bright?"

"No, I haven't," she replied. "I think it has something to do with the latitude. And of course, there's no pollution to speak of down here. Not yet, anyway."

Greg laughed. "You're not supposed to think about latitudes and pollution when you look up at the stars with a man, Nickie. You're supposed to say something soft and sweet in a breathy little voice."

"That's not my style."

"Obviously." He held her closer. "But don't they seem close enough to touch? Would you like me to pluck one out of the sky and give it to you?"

It was her turn to laugh. "No, thanks. It would be too hot to handle. Besides, it would throw the whole scheme of the universe out of kilter."

He sighed. "Well, we wouldn't want to do that, would we?" He released her waist and resumed his stride.

She ran to catch up with him. "Hey, it's dark out here, mister. Don't leave me stranded," she said. She sensed that she'd somehow left *him* stranded a moment ago, ridiculing his fancy of catching hold of a star for her.

"Don't worry, Nickie. I would never leave a beautiful woman stranded in the middle of the night." He took her hand.

Did he really think she was beautiful? Nicole wondered. Not that she was apprehensive about her looks. Thanks to evolution, heredity and a lucky combination of genes, she possessed the even features and slender figure that modern western culture considered attractive in women, and she accepted her looks for exactly what they were worth—face value. What Nicole wanted to know at that moment was if one particular man found her attractive and desirable. She quickly reminded herself that his opinion of her was of no importance whatsoever.

"Listen," he whispered, stopping again after they'd walked a few more yards.

Nicole could hear nothing for a moment, but then she picked up subtle rustling and chirping—a nocturnal melody of sounds, mysterious and a little frightening.

"What, Greg?" she whispered back. "What should I be hearing?"

"Shh." He pressed her head against his chest. "Do you hear it now?"

"Yes, I think I do," she said breathlessly, her lips brushing against his soft shirt. "What is it?"

"Phantom Carib drums sending a ghostly message," he said in a hushed tone.

"Really?" She shivered a little.

He chuckled. "Actually, sweetheart, it's my heart-beat. And the message it's sending is that I want you."

She twisted away from him. "You tricked me!"

She saw the flash of his smile. "Gotcha."

"You're such a pretender," she told him. "No wonder I don't trust you."

"But I'm not pretending. I do want you." Greg reached out and touched her cheek, then traced her jaw with his fingertip. He glided it down the column of her neck and across her collarbone, warming the smooth, cool surface of Nicole's skin. "I want you very much, Nickie."

He could feel the rise and fall of her chest beneath his fingertip as it grazed the low neckline of her dress. He placed his hand lightly on the top of her breast. He could feel her heat through the thin cotton material; he could smell her sweet, feminine scent in the still night air. And yes, he could hear her heart beating in time with his own—two phantom drums in the darkness.

Nicole didn't move. She couldn't. She wanted him, too. That was the simple truth of the matter, one she found very difficult to accept. How could she possibly want a man she distrusted? She was so disappointed in herself! She managed to shake her head slowly and then speak.

"Stop coming on to me, Chase."

How harsh her words seemed to him in the soft night. He took his hand away. "Is that what you call it when a man attempts to woo you, Nicole?"

"I call it hustling when you're the man doing it. I wasn't born yesterday, Chase."

"Don't you ever drop your guard?"

"Not when I'm around you, I don't."

"Perhaps that's just as well," he replied in a care-free tone that infuriated her. He said no more. Instead, he whistled a jaunty tune as he led her the rest of the way to her cottage.

"Sweet dreams," he wished her when they reached it. And without breaking stride he disappeared into the thick night, leaving Nicole feeling completely alone when she lost sight of his white shirt.

Chapter Six

Jane knocked on Nicole's cottage door first thing the next morning. "Rise and shine, dear girl!" she called. "Old Man Sun beat you to the punch hours ago."

Nicole smiled at the familiar childhood greeting and got out of bed to let her aunt in. The aroma of the rich Saint Sophian coffee hit her nostrils. "Oh, Jane, you didn't have to go to the trouble of bringing me breakfast," she said.

"No trouble, dear." Jane set the wicker tray she was carrying on a small round table by the window and opened the louvers. Golden bars of sunlight lighted up the room. "Marie baked banana bread especially for you this morning."

"Bananas plucked from a backyard plant, venture may I a guess, Madame Breck?" Nicole asked, imitating the housekeeper's lilting cadence and phrasing.

She felt odd, though, calling her aunt Madame Breck. Even after witnessing Toby's lovey-dovey performance last night, she still had trouble accepting him as Jane's husband.

"Yes, and this pineapple comes from the garden, too," Jane replied, pointing to a bowl of the fruit. "Marie also plucks papaya and guava and avocados from it. It's a veritable Garden of Eden."

It was on the tip of Nicole's tongue to remind Jane that there had been a snake in the Garden of Eden, but she kept that thought to herself. She sat down at the table and popped a juicy chunk of pineapple into her mouth. Ambrosia!

"Gregory tries to be as self-sufficient as possible," Jane went on, joining Nicole at the table and pouring the coffee. "He and Toby catch most of the seafood we eat, and he grows most of the vegetables and fruit." She put down the coffeepot and sighed deeply, contentedly. "Life here is so simple, Nicole. So good."

Nicole slowly buttered a piece of warm banana bread. "Don't you think you'll eventually get bored here, though, Jane?" she asked tentatively. "I mean, you're hardly the type to spend the rest of your life on a perpetual vacation. You worked so hard as director of the animal shelter and seemed to enjoy every minute of it."

"Yes, I did. It broke my heart when government funding was cut last year and it had to be closed. Too bad I hadn't won that sweepstakes then. I would have donated it all to the shelter to keep it going."

"You could go back to Vermont and start another one," Nicole suggested.

"No, I'm not going back, dear. I'm going *on* with my life. And Gregory has suggested a wonderful way for me to invest my time and money."

The morsel of moist bread in Nicole's mouth turned to cardboard. With great effort she swallowed it down. "Not his phony treasure-hunting venture, I hope!"

Jane looked dismayed. "Gregory Chase is not a phony, dear," she gently reprimanded. "His search for the Buenaventura is completely sincere. Why, he's devoted the last five years of his life to it. And since coming to Saint Sophia a few months ago, Toby has committed himself to helping him search."

Nicole was glad to hear Jane say that Toby had gotten involved only a short while ago. If that was true, it meant he hadn't been part of the Fitzwell scam. Even if it wasn't true, it still gave her leave to discuss the incident with Jane without seeming to implicate her husband. She immediately got up and found her purse. "Here, Jane, this is a copy of the article we were discussing last night." She took it out and offered it to her aunt.

But Jane picked up her coffee cup instead. "I have no interest in reading lies about my husband's cousin. Toby thinks the world of Gregory and so do I. He's been so kind and generous to me, dear." She smiled at Nicole. "And don't look so skeptical. He's not toadying up to me because I'm *rich*. It's his nature to be kind and generous. Ask Marie about Greg Mister, and she'll tell you how much he's contributed to the island."

"Marie works for the man! He probably coached her on exactly what to say."

"How absurd. Marie wouldn't lie if her life depended on it," Jane said, not in such a gentle tone this time. "You should get to know everybody a little better before you start tossing out accusations, Nicole."

"Yes, of course." She offered her aunt an apologetic smile. "That was wrong of me to say about Marie."

"And about Gregory."

Nicole's smile dissolved. "So you're going to invest money in his venture?"

"I would if he'd let me, but it so happens that he refused my offer."

"Then what was his wonderful suggestion?" she asked. "Does he want you to invest in his inn?"

Jane took a sip of coffee. "No, but he did promise to let me and Toby buy it from him if he ever decides to sell."

"He actually promised to let you give him money one of these days? You're right, Jane. He *is* kind and generous. Why, the man's a saint!" Nicole's voice was so heavy with sarcasm that she almost choked.

Her aunt shook her head. "I've never heard you talk this way about anyone before, dear. How can you dislike Gregory so much? You hardly know him."

"But I don't dislike him," Nicole countered, adding cream to her cup. "In fact, I find him perfectly charming. He's not only handsome, he's intelligent. And highly entertaining." She paused. "Not to mention sexy."

Jane's lips turned up. "You find him sexy, dear?"

"I said not to mention that."

"Now I'm beginning to understand, Nicole. It's your attraction to Gregory that's making you so hostile toward him."

"I'm not hostile," Nicole quickly denied.

"Well, distrustful, then." Jane patted her niece's arm. "Not every man you're attracted to will turn out to be a rat like Miles Avery, dear."

"Miles wasn't a rat, Jane. He was just confused about what he wanted in life."

"You still insist on coming to his defense." Jane shook her head. "Haven't you gotten over him yet?"

"Yes, of course I have. I haven't thought about him for years." Until recently, Nicole reminded herself, stirring her coffee thoughtfully. She'd begun thinking about Miles again after meeting Chase. Had her aunt touched on a truth she herself had been too blind to see? Was she suspicious of Chase because she felt susceptible when she was with him and was afraid of getting hurt again? No! she decided. She had good reasons for her suspicions and they had nothing to do with past hurts. She realized how difficult it would be to convince Jane of that until she had more proof, though.

Jane stood up. "We shouldn't be wasting such a beautiful morning talking about your ex-fiancé. Let's hit the beach!"

"You sound like a teenager, Aunt Jane. And it occurred to me yesterday that you look like one, too. Is there a fountain of youth on this island? Is that the secret of Saint Sophia?"

"Love is the secret, dear." Jane tossed back her braid. "Mine, anyway. Toby makes me feel like I'm the most desirable, beautiful woman in the world.

Whenever he so much as looks at me, he makes my heart flutter and my head spin.''

Hardly the frame of mind to make sound investment decisions, Nicole thought. Not that she wanted to be skeptical. It made her feel small-minded and mean-spirited to have such deep reservations about Toby. With all her heart Nicole wanted to believe that her aunt had found true love and happiness. "You don't have to entertain me, Jane," she said. "I'm sure you'd rather be spending time with Toby, and I have so much reading to do that I'll be perfectly happy alone.''

"Toby and Gregory are on a diving expedition this morning," Jane told her. "And although I made a promise that I wouldn't interfere with your work, I'm going to break it right now and drag you to the beach for at least an hour. So get into your swimsuit this instant.''

"Actually I forgot to pack one," Nicole said, a little abashed.

"You came all the way to the Caribbean without a swimsuit?" Jane's eyes widened in disbelief. "What on earth could you have been thinking of, Nicole?" She sighed. "Your work, no doubt. But it so happens that I have an absolutely perfect suit for you. It's never been worn. Toby bought it for me in Martinique, but frankly, dear, for all your compliments on my youthful appearance, I don't have the figure for a teeny bikini.''

"Well, neither do I!''

"Nonsense. You most certainly do. You don't have an extra ounce of flab on you.''

Nicole shrugged. "I don't have the inclination to wear one, then."

Jane smiled. "Fine. You'll simply have to sunbathe in the nude."

"That'll be the day," Nicole said.

Twenty minutes later Nicole and Jane were lying on a blanket spread over the soft, powdery sand of the Sea Rover's private beach. Nicole felt self-conscious in the bikini Jane had given her and kept tugging at the two skimpy red bands of cloth that barely covered her.

"Would you stop fidgeting?" Jane said. "There's no one around to see you. Besides, you're perfectly decent, dear."

"Easy for you to say," Nicole muttered, enviously eyeing Jane's modest one-piece suit. "I just don't feel comfortable wearing next to nothing after being bundled up in layers of clothes all winter."

"That reminds me," Jane said, digging into her straw bag and pulling out a plastic bottle. She tossed it to Nicole. "Put on some protective lotion. You do the front and then I'll get your back."

As Nicole was judiciously applying the lotion, she caught sight of Marie trudging toward them, coming from the direction of the house. She was carrying an umbrella, and when she reached them she stuck it into the sand and opened it.

"The first day you must be the most careful, Niece," she declared.

Nicole was touched by her caring gesture. "How kind of you, Marie. Thank you."

"And I've brought you something far better to apply upon your skin," Marie said, taking a brown glass bottle with a cork stopper from her apron pocket. "It was sent to you by Anabella Roseau, who also noticed your fairness when passing by you in a bus yesterday."

"That's the Carib lady who's a witch, isn't it?" Nicole asked, accepting the bottle with only the smallest display of hesitation.

Marie sniffed. "So she boasts. I place no faith in her claim, but do believe that Madame Roseau knows much of herbal medicines and balms. For that I trust her counsel."

"So do I," Jane said. "When I hurt my ankle Toby brought me straight to her. She wrapped some damp leaves around it, and I could feel the soothing effect immediately."

"Greg told me that a doctor looked at your ankle," Nicole said. "Not a *witch* doctor!"

Jane laughed. "Whatever she's called, she's a marvel."

"By the way, Madame Breck," Marie said. "You have a visitor awaiting you at the house."

"Who is it?"

Marie handed a card to Jane.

"Oh, dear," Jane said, getting up. "It's the lawyer from town. He wasn't suppose to arrive until lunchtime. Excuse me, Nicole. This won't take long. I'll be back shortly."

Nicole watched her walk away with Marie and couldn't help wondering why a local lawyer had come to see her aunt. Her suspicions surfaced again and she wished, as she had so many times lately, that Jane had never won all that money. Nicole simply wanted to be happy for Jane, sure that Toby loved her for herself

alone. Then there would be no reason to distrust Greg
Chase, either, Nicole thought wistfully. She could
lower her defenses and relax and enjoy herself with
him. That would be easy enough to do. Oh, yes, very
easy. His potent sexuality was hard to resist.

Nicole put a stop to such thoughts. It was just as
well she didn't trust the man. She might be disin-
clined to believe in romantic love, but she did believe
that a deep commitment was necessary before she had
a physical relationship with a man. Of that she was
certain. She was equally as certain that Chase wanted
the adventure of romance but no commitment whatsoever.

She moved under the shade of the umbrella, lay
down on her stomach, and covered her head with
Jane's big straw hat. As the sound of the lapping
waves, the sweet calls of exotic birds and the caress-
ing breeze soothed her, her concerns about her aunt
faded away for the moment and she drifted into sleep.

Nicole dreamed about being on a ship again.
Standing at the helm of a three-masted galleon, she
could see nothing ahead but clear skies and smooth
water. No pirate ships. No danger. Being the captain
of her own destiny and staying right on course gave her
great satisfaction. The sun beat down upon her back
as she steered the ship, but then she felt a sudden
coolness, followed by a light stroking. Only the caress
of the wind, she thought. But the strokes became more
sensual, causing a delicious melting deep within her.
She twisted her head and glimpsed the pirate standing
behind her. He'd invaded her ship once more, but she
simply couldn't make the effort to fight him off this

time. Not while his hands were doing such marvelous—

Nicole's eyes flew open and her buttery muscles went rigid. She threw off the straw hat and turned over.

"Chase!" she cried. He was kneeling beside her, naked to the waist, wearing cutoff jeans and his insufferable grin.

"Jane got tied up with some business and sent me down to the beach to check on you," he said. "Lucky I did. Now that the sun's higher, that silly umbrella isn't going to protect you."

"Were you pouring that stuff on me while I slept?" Nicole grabbed the brown bottle from his hand and sniffed. The contents smelled delightful, like crushed flowers. "What is it, anyway?"

"It's a love potion that I asked Madame Roseau to mix up for me."

"What?" Nicole squinted at him in the glaring sunlight. "Oh, I get it. You're teasing me again, Chase."

"Am I?" He took the bottle back and poured some of the fragrant oil into his palm. Slowly, methodically, he rubbed it into his golden chest and arms.

Nicole watched his every movement as if spellbound. Oh, he was teasing her now; there could be no doubt about it. His muscles gleamed as he coated them with the balm.

"There," he said. "The ritual has been completed. You are now in my power, Nicole Webster. My adoring love slave."

She couldn't help it. She had to smile. "You rogue," she said, tossing a handful of sand at his chest. Some of it stuck because of the lotion he'd applied. "You had me almost believing you for a moment there."

In a mere instant he was lying down, his long body stretched very close to hers on the blanket. "Believe me," he said, his voice low and husky as his eyes glided over every curving inch of her.

Nicole felt naked and vulnerable. She could feel the heat of his gaze burning into her body, even hotter than the sun. She sat up and wrapped her arms around her legs, covering herself as best she could. "I thought you were out diving." She somehow felt the need to let him know that she wouldn't have dressed, or rather *un*dressed this way if she'd known he'd be around.

"I was." He stretched lazily, muscles rippling. "No luck. Another false lead. The Buenaventura continues to elude me."

"Perhaps because it doesn't exist."

"Oh, she exists, all right," Greg replied breezily, impervious to her goading as always. "She's lying somewhere on the bottom of the sea, just waiting for me to discover her treasures after all these hundreds of years. Sort of like Sleeping Beauty waiting for Prince Charming to discover and claim her."

Was that the line he'd fed Mrs. Fitzwell? Nicole wondered. Finding his brown, gleaming body far too tempting to look at, she turned away and stared out at the sea.

"Don't keep turning your back on me, Nickie." Greg reached up and slid his hand down her bare, delicate spine.

She swiveled around to look at him again, shielding her eyes from the sun with her hand. "What's this great idea of yours about how Jane should invest her money?''

He sat up. "Who said I had one?"

"She did!"

"Then she must have told you what it was."

"The conversation got sidetracked. Before I could ask her about it again, she went off to meet with a lawyer. She has a perfectly fine lawyer back in Vermont. What does she need another one for?"

"Jane's home is Saint Sophia now," Greg reminded her. "Why shouldn't she have a local lawyer take care of her business?"

"What business?" Nicole demanded.

"What business is it of yours?" he countered.

"Your trick of always answering a question with another question is getting a little tiresome, Chase."

"Is it?" He grinned.

Nicole pushed herself up with a jerky, impatient movement. "You're impossible," she said, glaring down at him.

"And you're impossibly lovely," he replied, slowly raising his eyes from her bare feet to her face.

Nicole suffered his bold inspection without flinching, refusing to let him intimidate her with his challenging sexuality. "Had your fill?" she asked, placing her hand on her hip to demonstrate how perfectly cool and in control she felt.

"No, not really." He leaned back on his elbows and crossed his ankles. "Turn around for me, sweetheart."

She did. And then she walked away from him. Her gait was slow and easy as she strolled up the beach toward the house, but her heart hammered furiously with each step she took.

Greg shook his head as he watched her. As pleasing as it was, the view of Nicole's backside was becoming annoying. How many times had he let her get away with marching off like that? Well, this wasn't going to be one of those times, he decided, leaping up. He ran over the footprints she'd left in the sand and quickly caught up with her before she'd made it halfway back to the house.

"By the way, Nicole, do you know how to swim?" he asked her, as if there had been no break in their conversation.

"Like a fish," she replied.

Without another word he picked her up, carried her to the water, waded in as she struggled in his arms, and tossed her into an oncoming wave. She came up sputtering, railing at him in outrage, and it amused Greg to discover that the cool, prim Ms. Webster could swear like a sailor.

"Sorry, I couldn't resist the temptation," he said.

Nicole's outrage dissipated almost immediately and she welcomed the next wave with open arms and a smile. "It feels as warm as bathtub water," she said as the wave crashed against her chest. "It's absolute bliss."

Greg hadn't seen her smile like that before—with simple pleasure. And he'd never heard that laugh before as another wave almost knocked her down and a trill of surprised delight tinkled out of her throat. He wanted to hear her laugh like that again. And he wanted to be the cause of her surprised delight the next time she did.

"Come here," he said, wading toward her.

But she slapped the water hard, splashing him in the face, then dived into the next wave and swam away from him.

He had to actually strain a little to catch up with her. "Have you turned into a mermaid?" He was only half joking.

"I told you I could swim like a fish," she replied, treading water. "Fifty pool laps, four times a week. Keeps me in shape."

It certainly did, but Greg preferred to think of her as a sea nymph, not a sensible young woman who counted laps in a pool. They swam together for a while, like two dolphins on friendly terms with each other, and then caught a wave back to shore. When Nicole came out of the sea she was panting a little, but Greg sensed it was more from exhilaration than exertion.

"That was fun," she said. "I'm not even mad at you for throwing me in, Greg."

He hadn't expected her to be such a good sport about it. Water streamed from her sleek body, and her bikini was even more revealing wet. He felt his stomach muscles tighten. He'd wanted her from the moment he'd slid the garter up her thigh, but now it was more than a controllable hunger. Now it was a craving. He swore under his breath. He had no intention of falling in love with her.

"I'll go collect your blanket and things and bring them back to the inn," he said gruffly. "See you there."

Nicole headed back alone, puzzled by his gruff dismissal. She climbed the path leading up to the patio.

Hearing voices, she hesitated before going around the tall bougainvillea bushes that bordered it, wishing she had a robe to cover herself.

"I'll draw up the papers next week, Madame Breck," she heard a man say and guessed it was the lawyer from town.

Then she heard Toby's impatient voice. "Next week? Why not this week?"

"There's no big rush, is there, honey?" Jane asked him softly.

"But why wait?" Toby demanded. "It's what you want to do, isn't it, bunny?"

"I know this is what *you* want me to do," she replied. "But I need a little more time to think about it, Toby."

"As Madame Breck's attorney, I must counsel her to take her time before committing herself. This is a very large sum of money and I see no need for haste."

"I just want it all settled," Toby said irritably.

"And so it will be, Monsieur Breck. So it will be." The lawyer's chair scraped against the flagstones. "Good day."

"Wait. I'll walk you to your car," Toby said. Nicole heard another chair scrape and then footsteps receding.

But she hadn't heard any footsteps right behind her and gasped when she felt a big hand grasp her shoulder.

"Caught you," Greg whispered in her ear.

Chapter Seven

Nicole swung toward him, heart pounding, hands curled in tight fists. "Don't sneak up on me like that, Chase!"

"Looks like you were the one doing the sneaking, Nicole. Spies aren't welcome at the Sea Rover. Even pretty ones."

"I wasn't spying."

"You were eavesdropping."

Her face felt hot, her underarms prickly. "Not intentionally."

He cocked an eyebrow. "Did you *un*intentionally overhear anything interesting while you hid in the bushes?"

"I wasn't hiding, dammit!" She attempted to get past him but he blocked her way.

"Nicole, is that you?" her aunt called from the patio.

"Yes, Jane." She brushed against Chase, bare skin against bare skin, and her body tingled as she went around the hedge. "Greg and I went for a swim," she told her aunt as casually as she could.

Jane, seated alone at the glass and wrought iron table, smiled her gentle, trusting smile. "That's nice, dear. Would you like to join me for a glass of ice tea?" She raised her eyes to include Greg, following right behind Nicole, in her invitation.

"Sure," he replied. He put down the blanket and paraphernalia he'd collected and served himself from the pitcher on the table.

"I'll pass," Nicole said. She desperately wanted to talk to Jane alone but saw no way of getting rid of Chase, short of strangling him. "Would you come to my cottage with me, Jane? I'm not sure how to work the shower."

"Well, all right," her aunt replied, looking a little puzzled by Nicole's sudden incompetence.

"I'll show Nicole how," Greg volunteered.

He tilted back his head and drained his glass. She would definitely like to strangle him, Nicole thought again, fascinated by the tendons in his long, strong neck.

"Yes, Gregory can help you, dear," Jane said. "While I help Marie in the kitchen." She laughed lightly. "Rather, get in her way. She's going to teach me how to make conchburgers. Toby adores them! We'll have lunch in about an hour."

"Fine," Nicole said flatly.

Greg bowed formally and offered her his arm. She didn't take it.

On the way to the cottages, Nicole spotted Toby across the lawn, chatting with a black man dressed in a business suit and standing by a blue sedan.

"Jane's lawyer, I presume," she said.

"I get the feeling you presume too much," Greg replied.

His refusal to ever give her a straight answer exasperated her. "Let's stop beating around the bush, Chase."

"You prefer hiding behind one, don't you?"

"I don't regret overhearing what I did. I wish I'd heard more."

"Exactly what did you hear, Nicole?" His tone was calm, even disinterested.

"Enough to know that my aunt is soon going to be separated from her money if I don't step in and do something about it," she replied boldly.

She glanced at Chase. His lean face remained impassive. He said nothing until they reached her cottage. When he turned to look at her she could see that his eyes were cold green stones.

"Back off and stop meddling," he told her.

"I won't. I care too much about Jane."

"Or you care too much about her money."

"What?"

"You heard me. Relax, sweetheart. You won't get cut out completely. There's plenty to go around."

It took a moment for what he said to register. Nicole simply stared at him, frowning because his tone had been so harsh and cold. Then his words sank in and her arm shot up. She struck him across the face.

Her action shocked her. She hadn't slapped him hard but surely hard enough to sting. He didn't so much as blink. Rigid with tension, she waited for some kind of reaction. It came after a long, breathless moment. He smiled very slowly.

"The truth hurts," he said, rubbing his cheek.

Nicole could breathe again. "You wouldn't know the truth if it knocked you out, Chase! I'm sorry I hit you, but you deserved it." She reconsidered a moment, studying his smug, grinning face. "No, I'm not sorry." She ran up the steps and slammed the screen door behind her. It rattled on its hinges. She wasn't sorry about that, either.

He followed her in. It seemed he was always following her. "Did I say something to upset you, sweetheart?"

She grabbed her silky white robe from the closet and slipped it on. Her fingers trembled as she tied the belt around her waist. "Do you think everyone's like you, Chase?"

"It would be a far, far better world if they were." His tone was sardonic.

"A world I'd want no part of," Nicole responded, raising her chin. "And I want no part of my aunt's money, either. So don't try to cut some kind of slimy deal with me."

He reached out, took hold of the end of her belt, and rubbed the slippery material between his fingers. "What kind of deal did you have in mind, Nicole? How much money would it take to get you to leave Saint Sophia and stop making trouble?"

Nicole considered slapping him again but thought better of it. Tears of frustration burned her eyes. How could she possibly communicate with a man without morals, without principles, without a shred of integrity or conscience? They didn't even speak the same language. What frustrated her even more, what made the situation so intolerable at that moment, was that she still found him compellingly attractive. "You're trying to bribe me to leave?" she asked in horrified disbelief.

Greg saw the tears glisten in her stormy gray eyes. Either she was a damn good actress or he had truly offended her. Even if she was putting on an act and her motives for coming to Saint Sophia were mercenary, the tears melted Greg's resolve to get her to admit it. He regretted pressing her so hard.

"No, I don't really want you to leave, Nickie," he said in a gentler tone. "Forget I said all that, okay?"

She yanked her belt from his grasp and straightened her shoulders. "No, it's not okay and I won't forget. You're even worse than I thought you were, Chase. You're...you're...despicable!"

The image of one of Greg's favorite boyhood cartoon characters popped into his head—Daffy Duck spitting out the word "despicable." He did his best to contain his smile, but it returned.

"Get out!" Nicole shouted. She shoved at his chest. Again she was shocked by her own behavior. Shouting? Shoving? Why did this man reduce her to such unseemly behavior? She'd always been so proud of her control.

He put up his hands, palms toward her. "Listen, I'm sorry."

He meant it. Yet he couldn't help enjoying the rise he got out of her. She certainly always got one out of him. Right now he wanted to grab her, kiss her hard, tear off her robe and those two strips of red she wore under it. Desire for her gnawed at him, urging him to take what he wanted. No, he cautioned himself. That wasn't how to get what he really wanted from Nicole.

"Let me show you how to work the shower," he said, falling into his solicitous innkeeper role.

"I'll figure it out myself." She flung open the screen door. "You don't seem to appreciate how deeply you insulted me, Chase. I don't give a damn about Jane's money and I resent your insinuations."

"Good." He stepped out. "Now you know exactly how you make *me* feel, Nickie." He blew her a farewell kiss. "See you at lunch."

He always managed to get off the parting shot, Nicole thought. She really hated that.

The tepid shower she took didn't help cool Nicole down, and she could barely manage to be civil to Toby or Greg during lunch on the patio. She intended to find out what Toby had been pressing Jane to settle with her lawyer and hoped to have a private chat with her aunt after the meal. She had no appetite and picked at her conchburger, which tasted just like a fried clam patty.

"These are absolutely delicious," Toby said, forking another patty from the platter.

"I made them myself," Jane declared proudly.

His pale blue eyes widened in amazement. "You did, love? Why, you're as good a cook as Marie."

Jane laughed. "I'm glad she's not around right now to hear you say that."

"Well, it's true, honey," he insisted.

"You're so silly, bunny," Jane said.

As they wrinkled their noses at each other, Nicole looked away and rolled her eyes. Then she noticed that Greg was watching her. She'd felt him watching her during the meal and although she'd tried her best to ignore him, she found it impossible to do since he was seated directly across from her.

"Please tell me more about this sunken treasure you're searching for, Greg," she said with the utmost politeness.

"Oh, I wouldn't want to bore you, Nicole," he replied just as politely.

"But I'm sure it's simply fascinating," she said, her voice dripping with false cordiality.

"Oh, it is, dear!" Jane piped in. "Gregory, you must tell Nicole how you discovered that the Buenaventura went down off the coast of Saint Sophia. Nobody else has ever come up with that information."

Probably because it was *fabrication*, Nicole thought. Greg's parting words at the cottage hadn't been lost on her, though. Although she was still seething over his misinterpretation of her concern for Jane, she had to admit that he'd made a good point. She could possibly, just possibly be as wrong about him as he'd been about her.

"I really would like to hear more about it," she told him in a sincere voice. "Why do you continue to search for one particular ship?"

"Because she's the only one I'm interested in finding," he replied. "I never intended to become a treasure hunter. You might say that the Buenaventura found me rather than vice versa."

"She's become Greg's consuming passion," Toby interjected. "His family thinks he's a little crazy to have given up everything in order to find her. My uncle refers to him as the nutty professor."

Greg laughed. "Dad called me that even before I took off for Saint Sophia, Toby."

"That's true," his cousin agreed. He turned to Nicole. "Greg's old man could never understand why he went into teaching when he could have made so much more money in the family trucking business. So he sure doesn't understand what Greg's up to now."

Neither did Nicole, but she certainly wanted to. "If you haven't found a trace of the Buenaventura in all this time, what makes you still believe that it sank in this area?" she asked Greg.

"Oh, he's brought up plenty of stuff from his dives," Toby said. "Cannonballs. Pewter mugs and plates. Navigation instruments. Even bars of silver!"

Greg raised his hand to silence his cousin. "None of that matters, Tobias. All it proves is that some sixteenth-century Spanish ship went down around here, not that it was the Buenaventura. My only real proof is the seashell."

"A seashell?" Nicole asked, giving him an arch look.

"That's right, Nickie." He dug into the pocket of his white cotton pants, then tossed a shiny object into the air. He caught it in his fist and slowly opened his hand. "Take a look."

She leaned across the table and examined it closely. It was a seashell, all right, wrought in gold. It seemed to glow in Greg's palm.

"You can hold it if you'd like," he said.

She plucked it up, her fingertips grazing his palm. "It's beautiful," she said, cupping it gently in her own hand. "The design looks almost modern, though. Not at all like the antique Spanish jewelry I've seen in museums."

"You've got a good eye, Nickie." Greg smiled his approval. "No Spanish goldsmith designed that piece. It comes from another culture entirely, one Cortés had no qualms about wiping out when he came to the New World."

She looked at him with an astonished expression. "You mean Aztec?"

He nodded slowly. "I believe so."

"Gregory is convinced that the Buenaventura was bringing Aztec treasures back to Spain," Jane said.

"The rarest of treasures," Greg stated softly, his eyes never leaving Nicole's. "The conquistadors considered Aztec art pagan and melted down most of it."

She broke their gaze and looked back at the shell. It occurred to her that it could be a fake, not even real gold, let alone Aztec.

"Tell me, Chase. Where did you find this rare piece of art? At the local dime store?"

"Really, Nicole, what a thing to say!" Jane sent her a reproving look across the table.

But Greg only laughed. "Actually, I didn't even find it myself. One of the local fishermen did while we were in Vermont last week. He showed it to Marie and she called to tell me about it. That's why I rushed back here. I didn't want him to sell it to anybody but me."

"I'm sure a museum or collector would be willing to pay you a lot more than you paid a local fisherman if it's genuine," Nicole said.

"No doubt about it," Greg agreed. "I can't prove it's genuine, though. Not yet. I need to discover more Aztec artifacts to establish a provenance."

"So the real object of your quest isn't retrieving lost art. You want to make a profit from it!"

"Hey, what's wrong with that, Nicole?" Toby asked, his sunburned face becoming an even brighter red. "Why shouldn't Greg strike it rich when he finds the Buenaventura's mother lode?"

"I didn't mean to sound critical," Nicole said.

"You *always* sound critical," Toby told her. "Your nose has been out of joint ever since you came to Saint Sophia. If you find so much to disapprove of here, why don't you go back to Boston, lady?"

"Now, now," Jane said, patting her husband's hand. "That's no way to talk to Nicole."

"I'm sorry," he immediately apologized. But he looked at Jane, not her niece.

"Toby's right," Nicole said, her face red, too. "I was out of line. It seems I'm always saying things that you don't want to hear." She stood up abruptly. "Excuse me, please," she said with as much dignity as she could muster. "I'm going to take a walk on the beach."

No one uttered a word to detain her.

Hands jammed in the pockets of her white shorts, shoulders hunched in dejection, Nicole plodded along the tide's edge and contemplated what she should do next. Obviously she wasn't wanted here, and her cozy apartment back in Boston called to her. How nice it would be, she thought, to be there right now, at her desk working undisturbed, a steaming cup of tea at her elbow. She imagined herself taking a sip of it, glancing out the window to see snow falling, feeling as snug as a bug in a rug. She had such a good, productive life back in Boston—her research work was satisfying and occasional lecture tours kept her from getting into a rut. Yet there were times when she would feel all the love in her and wish she had someone to share it with. Sometimes she wished for a man to love. Sometimes she wished for a child. Sometimes she would pull out all the stops and wish for both.

At the present moment, though, all Nicole yearned for was to return to Boston. Jane, wrapped up in Toby, had little time for her. If she turned around and went back to the inn to announce her immediate departure, Nicole was sure that her aunt, after a few "Oh, dear, oh dear," protests, would help her pack her bag with great relief. Everybody would feel relieved to be rid of her! Yet as uncomfortable as Nicole felt in her role as the unwanted guest, she was determined to remain at the Sea Rover until she knew what both Toby and Greg were up to.

Money, Nicole thought, shaking her head. How it complicated life. It changed perspectives and relationships. Now that Jane was a millionaire three times over, Nicole couldn't feel the same about her. She didn't love her aunt more or less because of it, but she couldn't help feeling differently about their relationship. She now felt obligated to somehow guard over Jane and defend her interests. Yet every time she expressed concern, Jane took it as an insult to her husband and her own good judgment.

Nicole recalled the time when their positions had been reversed and Jane had distrusted the love of *her* life. Oh, how she'd resented it whenever Jane had made the slightest hint that Miles was less than perfect. So she could understand Jane's attitude now. That didn't make her feel any better, though, or any less of an intruder. It went against Nicole's nature to impose herself where she wasn't wanted.

For the second time that day she felt tears of frustration burn her eyes. She bowed her head and watched the waves lap at the shore. And since no one was around to see her, she gave herself permission to have a good cry. She watched the tears fall from her eyes and plop into the foam. Salt into salt, she thought. At that particular moment it seemed like a very deep thought.

"Hey. You okay?" The voice was low and quiet. The arm that suddenly wrapped itself around her hunched shoulders was long and strong. And warm.

"Chase! Didn't I ask you to stop sneaking up on me?" Nicole inhaled a mighty sniff, which she was sure discounted her attempt to sound tough.

Greg hugged her closer and fell into step with her. "Toby didn't mean to hurt your feelings, sweetheart. He feels terrible right now and so does Jane."

She sniffed again. "So do I."

"Then that makes four of us, because I feel terrible, too. I was way too hard on you during our talk before lunch. I made some pretty nasty innuendos. You were right to give me a smack."

"No, that was wrong. But you were so off base, Greg!"

"I'm beginning to think I was, too. That's why I came down to the beach to talk to you. I don't want you to get the idea that we want you to go away."

Nicole choked out a laugh through her tight throat. "Why would I get an outlandish idea like that? Just because you tried to bribe me to leave, and Toby suggested it in no uncertain terms?"

"Oh, that's an old island custom." He gave her shoulder a squeeze. "See, when we want someone to stay on Saint Sophia, we say just the opposite. Maybe that's why we don't have too many tourists down here. They don't understand our rudeness is really a convoluted form of cordiality."

"Good try, Greg. But I'm not buying it." His attempt to appease her with a joke made Nicole feel a little better, though.

"I just hope you're not buying the next plane ticket out of here, Nickie. We really do want you to stick around."

"Sure, like gum on a shoe."

Greg grinned. "I couldn't have phrased it better myself." He kissed the top of her bowed head, and the light graze of his lips on her hair warmed Nicole from her head to her toes. "How would you like to go to a wild party with me?" he asked her. "You'll see things you never imagined were possible."

What on earth was he inviting her to? Nicole wondered. An orgy?

She shook her head. "I'm not much of a swinger, Greg." And she didn't like the idea that he could be one.

"I promise you'll really enjoy yourself once you get into the swim of things, Nickie."

"I don't think so. Where's this party being held?" she asked, hoping it wasn't at the Sea Rover.

"Underwater," he replied. "That's where my most exotic, flamboyant friends congregate. I want you to come snorkeling with me."

She smiled, relieved and delighted. "It's something I've always wanted to do."

"Come on then." He turned her around. "Let's go change and get the diving gear. We're going to another world, Nickie."

She picked up her pace to match his, perfectly willing to let him take her there.

"All we have to do is swim out twenty yards or so, and we'll be in one of the most beautiful natural sea gardens in the West Indies," Greg told Nicole when they arrived at the diving site, a deserted cove about a mile's hike up the coast from the inn. "I discovered it purely by accident." He looked out to the sea. "If I never find the Buenaventura, at least I found that."

It was the first time Nicole had heard him sound less than optimistic about his venture. He dipped a diving mask into the calm, shallow water and handed it to her.

"Spit on the inside of the lens," he ordered and grinned when she looked surprised. "Prevents it from fogging," he explained. "Rub the saliva around and then rinse the mask again."

She did exactly as she was told and fitted the mask to her face.

Greg secured the strap around her head. "Comfortable?" he asked. She nodded and he attached the snorkel to the strap. "Now put on your fins," he told her.

When she bent to the task her pert breasts almost escaped from the scant confines of her bikini top, and Greg took in a sharp, appreciative breath.

"Well?" she asked, straightening up after she'd slipped on her fins. "What next?"

"Now you take off your swimsuit."

"I hardly think that's necessary." Nicole put her hands on her hips and attempted a haughty look, which was difficult to carry off, wearing a face mask. Flippers didn't much help the effect, either.

"You're too smart for me, Nickie. Most of the other women I bring here fall for that one."

Nicole knew it was absurd, even stupid, to feel disappointed, but she couldn't help it. "You mean you bring all your female guests at the inn here to...snorkel?"

Was that a note of jealousy he detected in her cool voice? Greg wondered. "Well, certainly not *all* of them," he replied breezily, then waded into the crystal-clear water. He gestured for Nicole to join him.

She didn't budge from the shore. "Only the ones who prefer swimming in the buff, I suppose."

Greg considered teasing her some more but decided against it. "Only you," he replied.

Hoping that was true, she joined him in the water.

"Before we swim out to the coral reefs, I want you to practice in waist-deep water for a few minutes," he told her. "Once you get used to breathing through the snorkel, you can relax and enjoy the show below." He had her lie facedown in the water, arms at her sides. "Move your legs slowly up and down," he instructed. "And keep your toes pointed back."

Greg watched her glide through the water, her long legs moving rhythmically, her round bottom bobbing, and his body stirred at the sight. Lust, pure and simple, he thought, but in the next instant admitted to himself that what he felt for Nicole was more complicated than that. It was more than her body he wanted, and that was what bothered him so much. Becoming emotionally involved with Nicole would be a big mistake for both of them.

She stopped floating and stood upright in the water. "How am I doing?" she asked him.

"Beautifully," he replied, his voice a little husky.

"Am I ready to crash that wild party?"

He nodded. "Just try to keep your fins under the water instead of letting them break the surface. The splashing scares away the fish. They're pretty friendly, though. Almost tame, in fact."

He went back to shore and put on his own gear.

"Don't touch the coral. It could cut your skin," he warned her when he returned. "Follow me and stay close to me at all times."

"At all times," she repeated softly, her eyes wide and luminous behind the glass lens.

Greg felt the urge to kiss her then. But their masks and snorkels would have gotten in the way. Just as well, he thought. He wouldn't have been satisfied with one kiss.

Chapter Eight

Greg led Nicole to the magnificent coral reefs, the habitat of tropical fish of every shape, size and hue. It was a world of silence, peace and beauty that Greg knew well. He found it even more beautiful with Nicole floating beside him, skimming her slender body against his and sometimes squeezing his arm to communicate her pleasure at what she saw.

Sunlight pierced the water and lighted the rosy coral as schools of fish scurried past. Once Nicole became acclimated, she grew almost as nimble as a fish herself, diving to the bottom with Greg and following him around the reefs. Once again he admired her swimming ability and found himself thinking how nice it would be to always have Nicole beside him, his companion, his mermaid, his mate. He immediately cut off such thoughts, reminding himself that they weren't half so companionable out of the water.

When they returned to shore Nicole was in high spirits. "That was the most thrilling experience I've ever had!" she told Greg as they stripped off their masks and fins. Her face was flushed, her eyes glowed. "I can't imagine doing anything that could top it."

Greg certainly could. How he adored the sight of her wet, glistening body.

"I swear one of those fish smiled at me, Greg. Sort of a silly grin like the one you're wearing now. Bright blue."

"My grin is bright blue?"

She laughed as if he'd said the cleverest thing possible. She was on a natural high. "No, the fish was, of course. Do you know which one I mean?"

"Probably a parrot fish." And Greg knew that he would never be able to see a parrot fish again without thinking it had smiled at Nicole.

Always intent on acquiring new information, she asked what the yellow and black fish were called.

"French angel," Greg said.

It pleased her that he knew about things that she didn't. "And the dark blue ones with diamond spots?"

"Jewel fish," he told her.

"Lovely," Nicole said.

"Yes, lovely," he agreed, noticing how droplets of water clung to her body like jewels. He would have liked nothing better than to lick them off, tasting the salt on her skin. Instead, he tossed her a towel.

"And what were those fish that glowed called?" she asked. "They were emerald with luminous silver stripes."

"Triggerfish," he replied, although he was having trouble remembering his own name as he watched Nicole rub herself down with the towel.

"Triggerfish," she repeated. "Such an ordinary name for such gorgeous creatures."

"You're right. They should be renamed Nicole Webster fish."

She began to laugh, assuming he was teasing her, but when she saw the look of avid desire in his eyes the laughter caught in her throat and the towel slipped from her hands. She knew what he intended to do as he slowly moved toward her, and she couldn't allow it to happen again.

She cleared her throat and started talking fast. "Did you know, Greg, that mouth-to-mouth kissing developed more in western cultures than in eastern ones? I haven't yet come up with a satisfying hypothesis of why that is, but I do know that—"

"Shut up," he said softly.

And Nicole suddenly found herself captured in his arms, her breasts pressed against his bare chest. He grasped a hank of her wet hair and pulled her head back, then kissed her with a greedy urgency that took her breath away. She melted against him, feeling the rough material of his cutoff jeans against her bare belly and thighs.

"Open your mouth to me," he commanded.

And she did because she felt powerless to refuse him. He tasted like sunlight, like salt, like the very essence of life. She became greedy for him, too, for the absolute pleasure she knew he could give her. Their tongues played together and she had the same wonderful, weightless sensation as when they'd dived in the sea together.

He lifted his mouth from hers and smiled. "Do you have a hypothesis about *that*?" he murmured.

Nicole broke away from his embrace and shook her head to clear it. "A universal courtship gesture," she managed to reply in a shaky voice. "Which bypasses the thinking part of the brain and goes straight to the primitive neural center."

Greg groaned. "I shouldn't have asked."

What he shouldn't have done, he knew, was kiss her. His primitive neural center was going haywire right now. Green lights were flashing. All systems were go. She was giving him the go-ahead herself, whether she realized it or not—and the outline of her hardened nipples was visible through her thin bikini top.

He reached out for her. She backed away. "Don't," she said. "Please don't touch me again."

"But you want me to." He smiled, coaxing her. "You want me to make love to you."

"The thinking part of my brain doesn't."

"Then we'll bypass it again." He opened his arms to her. "Come here, Nickie."

"No!" She ran past him and down the beach.

Nicole stopped running because no one was chasing her. She felt such a fool! She was sure that Greg thought her one, too. Why had she allowed him to kiss her like that? Why had she kissed him back like that? She was a mature, sensible woman, not some capricious little flirt. She glanced over her shoulder and saw him walking toward her, his gait relaxed, unhurried. She waited for him to catch up.

"Here," he said gruffly, handing her a towel. "Cover your back before it gets burned."

"Thanks." She offered him a little smile as she wrapped the towel around her shoulders.

He frowned back. "Dammit, you didn't have to run away from me, Nicole. What the hell did you think I was going to do? Attack you?"

"No, of course not." It was odd, she thought, that for all she distrusted him, she sensed with every fiber of her being that he would never violate her physically. "I suppose I was running away from my own inclinations," she admitted.

He laughed sharply. "That could get to be exhausting if you make a habit of it." He paused to pick up a stranded starfish and toss it back into the sea. "Do you?"

"Do I what?"

"Make a habit of running away from men you're attracted to."

"No, just you, Greg."

"Hmm. I don't know if I should feel complimented or insulted."

"Maybe both."

They walked the rest of the way back to the Sea Rover without speaking, and the incoming tide washed away the footprints they'd left side by side in the sand.

Nicole dressed carefully for dinner that evening. She had to dress carefully because she'd managed to get sunburned, after all, and her skin was sensitive. Luckily she'd packed a black silk halter dress, which left her hot, flaming back bare. When she arrived on the veranda, she was glad to see that Jane and Toby were already there. She didn't want to be alone with Greg. At the same time she was disappointed that he hadn't arrived yet.

Toby bounded from his chair and hurried across the porch, bumping into a big terra-cotta planter containing lilies, to meet her halfway. "Hi, Nicole. You look great," he said with hearty friendliness.

He reminded her of a puppy eager to make amends for misbehaving. She smiled, touched by his awkward affability. "Thanks, Toby."

"Listen, I'm really sorry about snapping at you during lunch today."

"Forget it," she said. "I have."

"No, I want to explain. See, I get overly defensive about Greg because he used to fight a lot of battles for me when I was a kid. He understood my problem and didn't let the other kids make fun of me."

"Your problem?"

"I'm an epileptic. It's not really a problem anymore. It's been under control with medication for years now."

"That's good." Nicole smiled back at him. His sweet, lopsided smile seemed so sincere and open. Yet the conversation she'd overheard earlier still bothered her. What had Toby been pressing Jane to sign as soon as possible?

"Well, I'm glad we cleared the air," he said. "Since I'm, supposed to be the bartender around here, let me get you a drink."

"All right. What are you and Jane drinking?"

"Passion punch, as usual," Jane called from the rattan sofa, rattling the ice in her glass.

Nicole joined her aunt. They hadn't seen each other since lunch. "Maybe I'd better not have any punch," she said. "Greg warned me how potent it was and after a day in the sun, it's probably not a good idea for me to have a strong rum drink."

Jane frowned. "But there's no rum in this mixture, dear. Just fruit juices. Because of his condition, Toby can't drink alcoholic beverages." She laughed. "Gregory must have been teasing you."

Nicole accepted the glass Toby offered her and sat down beside her aunt. When she took a sip of the punch it tasted pleasant but bland, and she realized that it had been Greg's presence that had had such a heady effect on her the night before. Where was he? she wondered.

Toby sat down across from them. "Did you do anything special this afternoon?" he asked Nicole.

"Greg took me snorkeling in a glorious coral sea garden."

"He took you there?" Toby looked surprised. "That's his secret place. Greg won't show anybody where it is, not even me or Jane."

Nicole felt warm all over. It could have been the sunburn, she thought. Or the knowledge that Greg had shared something very special with her. Where *was* he? she wondered again.

"We had a wonderful afternoon, too," Jane said. "We went birding."

"Really?" Nicole did her best to look interested although she'd never shared her aunt's enthusiasm for bird-watching, however much Jane had tried to foster it when she was a child.

"We spotted a motmot," Toby said.

Jane smiled indulgently. "No, honey, that was a jacamar."

"You're wrong, bunny," her husband replied. "I know a motmot when I see one. It looks like a cross between a bee eater and a kingfisher."

"So does a jacamar. But it's much smaller than a motmot."

"Bunny, you barely got a glimpse of the bird. I had a much longer look and it was definitely a motmot!"

Nicole's attention had wandered, but she focused on Jane and Toby again when she realized that they were having a lover's spat. About birds, no less!

"It was a jacamar," Jane insisted, raising her gentle voice ever so slightly.

"Maybe you need a new set of binoculars," Toby suggested.

"Maybe you need a new set of eyes," Jane retorted.

"Sounds like the honeymoon is over," a deep quiet voice interjected.

Greg came up the veranda steps, grinning, and Nicole's heart jumped at the sight of him. He was wearing a cream linen suit, rumpled yet elegant, a light yellow dress shirt, and a beautiful blue silk tie. The sight of him took her breath away.

"Are these two brawling about birds again?" he asked her.

"Not exactly brawling," she managed to answer.

"The only thing they ever argue about is the identification of their feathered friends," he told her. "I think they do it because they have such a good time making up later."

Jane tittered. "Oh, Gregory, that's not true."

"Well, we *do* have a good time making up," Toby allowed. He bent and kissed his wife's cheeks. "Your binoculars are just fine, Mrs. Breck."

"And I adore your eyes, Mr. Breck," Jane replied, gazing up at him.

Meanwhile Nicole was gazing at Greg. Why was he dressed so formally? Surely not to impress her. "All you need is a panama hat to look like an aristocratic plantation owner," she observed.

"Lord, that's the last thing I want to look like!" He tugged at the knot in his tie.

"Gregory is dining with the governor this evening," Jane informed her niece.

"One of many guests," Greg hastened to add. "He's invited half the island."

"No, he hasn't, Gregory. Only those who contributed so much time and effort to modernize the Saint Sophia hospital." Jane turned to Nicole. "Gregory headed the fund-raising committee."

Nicole did her best not to look too surprised. "I'm impressed."

"Don't be," Greg said. "I figured that if I ever got sick, it would be nice to have a decent hospital to go to."

"Oh, stop pretending that self-interest motivated you," Jane told him and turned to Nicole. "He's also involved in raising money for a home for the aged poor."

"Hell, that's self-interest, too, since I may end up there one day," Greg declared gruffly. "I may spend the rest of my life on this island searching for the Buenaventura.''

Toby laughed. ''I can just see you fifty years from now, your old bones creaking as you hoist yourself over the gunwale.''

''Maybe by that time someone will have invented a bifocal diving mask,'' Greg joked.

''But you must have given yourself a time limit,'' Nicole said. ''And once you've reached it you'll give up your search, won't you?''

''Give up?'' Greg smiled grimly. ''No, Nicole. I'll never do that.''

''You would find the Buenaventura a lot quicker if only you'd let me lend you some money to expand the search, Gregory,'' Jane said.

''Too much of a gamble,'' he replied curtly.

''But I can afford to risk it,'' Jane insisted. ''I have plenty to spare.''

''Not for long, you won't. Not if you go along with my suggestion,'' Greg said.

Nicole tensed but remained silent. It took a great deal of effort.

''That's right,'' Toby said. ''The whole point of Greg's plan is to relieve you of the weight of your millions, Janey.'' He picked up the pitcher of punch. ''Care for a drink, Greg?''

He glanced at his watch. ''No, thanks. I'd better get going or I'll be late. I hope the governor doesn't make one of his endless speeches tonight.''

''He'll probably ask you to make one,'' Toby said.

Greg winced. ''The only one I know starts out, Welcome, ladies and germs, and goes downhill from there.''

Everybody laughed except Nicole, who sat rigid and stunned beside Jane. She couldn't believe what she'd just heard Greg declare and Toby agree to. She couldn't believe they they'd discussed divesting Jane of her fortune right in front of her. And now her aunt was laughing as if nothing ominous had transpired at all.

"Good night, Nicole," Greg said, taking up her cold hand. "I'm sorry I can't join you for dinner this evening."

She couldn't utter a word. She just stared at him.

"You look beautiful in black," he said. "The color makes your gray eyes look silver. Like the stripes on those fish we saw today." He noticed her troubled expression. "Are you all right, Nickie? You didn't get too much sun, I hope."

"Maybe I did," she said in a weak voice.

"Everybody gets too much their first few days here." He offered a sympathetic smile. "Just take a couple aspirin and go to bed early." He said goodbye to Jane and Toby and then strolled off the porch.

"Greg's going to miss a great meal," Toby said. "We're having crayfish tonight. Hope you like crayfish, Nicole."

"Oh, she'll love the way Marie prepares it," Jane said. She glanced at her niece. "What's wrong, dear? Are you feeling ill?"

Nicole couldn't keep up this polite charade a moment longer. "It seems something *is* terribly wrong, Jane!" She glared at Toby. "I'd like to know what you and Chase are up to, with all your blatant talk about separating my aunt from her money. Are you going to level with me, Toby?"

"Yes." He leaned toward her and rested his elbows on his knees. "The first thing you should know is that I lied to Jane in the beginning."

Nicole's heart sank.

"I know I should have been completely honest with her before we got married, but I was too afraid of losing her."

"You could never lose me." Jane told him softly.

"What did you lie about?" Nicole asked him.

"My father. He's not a geophysicist. Heck, I'm not even sure what that is, but it sounded impressive. He's not in India, either. He's in prison."

"Income tax evasion," Jane put in.

"That's too bad," Nicole said. "But it's no reflection on you, Toby. Did you lie to my aunt about anything else?"

"No. But after I told her I was an epileptic and that I had no big career ambitions, I didn't want to push my luck. I figured that telling her about my father would have been the third strike against me."

"None of that matters to me, love!" Jane insisted.

Since her aunt didn't care about it, none of that really mattered to Nicole, either. She was far more concerned about the present state of affairs.

"What plan have you and Greg cooked up to relieve Jane of millions, as you so delicately put it?" she asked him.

"Actually, Greg's the one who came up with it," he replied.

That was exactly what bothered Nicole most. "Go on," she said.

"Jane and I want to spend the rest of our lives together on this island. The simple life-style suits both of us. We feel at peace here."

"I knew I belonged here the moment I arrived," Jane said. "It's a bird-watcher's heaven."

"Jane's made me an ardent birder, too, even though I didn't know the difference between a motmot and a jacamar before I met her."

"You still don't, honey," Jane said sweetly.

"Please!" Nicole begged. "Let's not get into that again."

Toby nodded. "The thing is, we can't expect Saint Sophia to remain so pristine and undeveloped forever," he continued. "The government is encouraging more industrial development. Tourism, too. The roads will have to be improved and an airport built to accommodate jet planes."

"And we've heard that a consortium of European investors is buying up prime land with the intention of building hotels and golf courses on it," Jane added.

"Land prices have started to skyrocket, and that's why I want Jane to move fast, before it's too late."

Nicole still didn't understand what he was leading up to. "You want Jane to invest in a hotel complex?"

Jane laughed. "Just the opposite, dear. Gregory suggested that I buy as many acres of land as I can for a bird sanctuary, and that's what Toby wants me to do."

"A bird sanctuary?" Nicole repeated.

"Well, it makes perfect sense, doesn't it?" Toby said. "Jane and I don't need much money to live here, so why shouldn't most of it be used to preserve what we most value? I want Jane to bequeath the sanctuary to the Saint Sophian people as a national park, her gift to future generations of islanders."

"*Our* gift, honey," Jane corrected. "What's mine is yours."

Toby shook his head. "No, I've never seen it that way. I've always felt uncomfortable about your money, Janey. But I won't if you put it to good use. Besides, I think we'd both really get a charge out of running a bird refuge."

"It would be a dream come true," she agreed.

Toby turned to Nicole. "There's an ideal tract of land for sale right now. If Jane hesitates closing the deal for much longer, the owner may get a better offer from that European investment group. And I don't think she's going to be too happy seeing all that natural vegetation cleared for a golf course."

"Oh, I would hate that to happen," Jane said. "It's the habitat of so many rare species. But this has all happened so quickly, and I'm not the sort to rush into anything. I'm so afraid of making the wrong decision."

Nicole cleared her throat. "Well, Jane, you rushed into marrying Toby, didn't you?" She paused. "And that was the best decision you could have made." She looked at Jane's husband with a new respect and appreciation. "I've misjudged you, Toby, although I had no right to judge you at all. Will you forgive me?"

He nodded and his smile spoke for itself.

Because of her sunburn, Nicole had trouble sleeping that night. She went outside and sat on the porch step. It was warm enough to be comfortable in her cotton nightgown, and a light breeze soothed her smarting back and shoulders as she stared up at the stars. Despite her discomfort, she felt at peace for the first time since she'd come to Saint Sophia. She didn't have to worry about her aunt anymore. She knew Jane would find great satisfaction in her conservation project. And Greg had come up with the idea!

She had no reason to distrust him now, no reason to hold back her feelings for him. She let them flow through her in a sweet rush. She wanted him as she'd never wanted a man before. How delicious it felt to be able to admit that to herself without reservation. She threw back her head and smiled at the twinkling stars.

When she saw him coming up the path, his light suit bright in the moonlight, she called softly to him.

Greg climbed the porch steps and sat down beside her. "It's way past midnight. What are you doing up?"

"Waiting for you," she said. She had been hoping to hear his footsteps through the night sounds of crickets and whistling tree frogs for the last hour. She kissed his cheek. "Toby and Jane told me about the bird sanctuary. It's a wonderful idea, Greg."

"It seemed the perfect solution to the problem."

"The problem?"

"The money, Nickie. Frankly, I think your aunt is very naive when it comes to dealing with finances. And Toby... well, let's face it. He's no financial wizard. It's not that he's stupid, mind you. It's just that he thinks with his heart, not his head. I've always felt protective toward him."

"The two honey bunnies," Nicole said softly, shaking her head. "What a pair!"

"They'll be happy together here in Saint Sophia," Greg said.

"Yes, I believe that now. They want the same thing. But why didn't you tell me what they planned to do when I asked you about the lawyer, Greg?"

"That was up to Jane, not me. I'm relieved to hear that you don't object, though."

"Why would I object?"

"Well, that's pretty obvious, isn't it? You and your father are Jane's closest relatives."

"Oh, I get it. You thought we wanted to keep all that money in the family."

"It crossed my mind."

"No, Greg. All we were concerned about is that she didn't get swindled out of it."

"So now that you know that Toby and I aren't out to get her millions, you can stop worrying and go home."

"Go home?" Nicole's happiness suddenly dimmed. "Is that what you want me to do?"

Greg didn't answer for a moment. It seemed like a century to Nicole. "You can stay as long as you want."

But what did *he* want? Pride wouldn't allow her to ask again. "How did your dinner at the governor's go?" she asked instead.

"He offered me a position on his staff. I was pretty flattered."

"Did you accept?"

"How could I? I already have a full-time job."

Nicole laughed. "Searching for the Buenaventura, you mean?"

"Yes, that's exactly what I mean." His tone was testy. "What's so damn funny about that?"

His rebuke stung and Nicole remained silent. How strange, she thought, that he'd never taken offense all the times she'd intentionally tried to anger him, and now, when offending him was the last thing she wanted to do, he'd snapped at her. Neither of them spoke for a while, and the sound of crickets seemed to become louder and louder, almost a shriek in Nicole's ears.

"I'm sorry," they finally said in unison. And then they both laughed awkwardly.

"I wasn't trying to make fun of your search, Greg."

"But you can't understand why I'm wasting my life away down here?"

"It's your life," she hedged.

He stood up and she was sure that he was leaving because she'd offended him again. But he extended his hand. "Let's go inside, Nickie," he said. "I'll tuck you in and tell you a bedtime story."

She took his hand and he pulled her to her feet. They stood in the moonlight, staring at each other for a long moment. "Yes, tuck me in," she said softly.

Chapter Nine

The little lamp on the wicker night table gave Nicole's room a soft, mellow glow. Greg went to the bed, fluffed up the pillows and placed them against the headboard.

"Climb in, sweetheart," he said, turning down the covers. When she did, he smoothed the light blanket and sat at the edge of the bed by her feet. "Now where should I begin?" he wondered aloud.

A bemused smile lifted the corners of Nicole's lips. He really was going to tell her a bedtime story. The idea charmed her completely. "How about starting off with 'Once upon a time'?" she suggested.

He nodded. "Once upon a time there was a college professor who should have been content. He taught a subject that fascinated him—"

"Spanish colonial history?" Nicole interrupted.

Greg pretended to look amazed. "That's right. Have you heard this story before?"

"No, it was just a lucky guess." She adjusted the pillow behind her back. "Why wasn't he content?"

Greg shrugged. "Who knows? He had everything going for him. He was twenty-eight years old, teaching at an Ivy League university—"

"Harvard?"

"No, Yale. But I can change it to Harvard if you'd prefer."

Nicole shook her head. "Stick to the truth. I promise I won't interrupt anymore."

"And he was engaged to a beautiful princess," Greg continued.

"Was he?" Nicole asked, immediately breaking her promise. "But they didn't marry and live happily ever after, or he wouldn't be alone in Saint Sophia now."

"I never said this story had a happy ending, Nickie."

"Well, *did* they marry?" she demanded.

Greg sighed. "No. The princess broke their engagement and called the man a fool."

"Maybe she was a witch in disguise," Nicole couldn't help herself from suggesting.

"No, Nickie. She was just a very practical princess. She couldn't understand why a man would give up his career to go chase after a dream." Greg's voice turned wistful. "I asked her to come with me, but she refused. I asked her to wait for me, but she wouldn't. It seems princesses aren't accustomed to making compromises."

"What was her name?" Nicole asked, tired of hearing this love in Greg's life referred to as a princess.

"Barbara. She wanted to settle down with someone who had a secure job, and so she opted for a stable future rather than a romantic adventure. Three months after I came down here she sent me an invitation to her wedding." He laughed sharply. "Barbara didn't waste much time finding herself another Prince Charming."

"But you were the one who left," Nicole pointed out.

"I always intended to go back to her, though! I asked her to give me one year, that's all. But after she married I had no reason to go back. So I invested every penny I had in the Sea Rover, in order to make some sort of living here until I found the Buenaventura."

"I wonder," Nicole said.

"Wonder what?"

"If Barbara *had* waited for you, would you have given up the search after the year was up?"

Greg raised his thick, dark eyebrows. "That's a very perceptive question."

"And what's the answer to it?"

"I really don't know," he admitted. "Most likely I would have. I'm not a cad. I wouldn't ask a woman to wait for me and then not fulfill my end of the bargain."

"You mean you would have returned more out of obligation than desire?"

"Oh, Nickie, who knows?" He took off his tie and threw it aside. "It didn't happen that way."

"Why didn't you fly back to Connecticut and try to win Barbara back the moment you received her wedding invitation?"

"Because I'd already developed a great passion for my Saint Sophia mistress by then."

Nicole's heart tightened. "You neglected to mention you had a mistress here, Greg."

"No, I haven't." His slow, teasing smile inched across his wide mouth. "In fact, I've mentioned her by name many times. She's called Buenaventura, and she's become a very time-consuming, elusive mistress."

Nicole felt a surge of relief followed by a sharp pang of jealousy, which surprised her. It made no sense to be jealous of a sunken ship. Yet it somehow made perfect sense, too. "Please go on with your story, Greg," she said. "I think we got sidetracked."

"You're right. We did." He got up, took off his jacket, rolled up the sleeves of his shirt, and sank onto the bed again. "Now where did I leave off?"

"The princess is out of the picture."

"Actually I never meant to bring her into it. I didn't intend to tell you a story about losing Barbara. Maybe I should start all over again. In the sixteenth century this time."

"Is this a reincarnation story?" Nicole asked, tucking up her legs and hugging her knees. "Are you going to tell me about the time you were a Spanish conquistador in a past life?"

"If there is such a thing as reincarnation, I hope I wasn't a conquistador. They were ruthless men, Nickie. My story is about a man who came to the New World in search of knowledge, not gold. He was a scholar and a gentleman and his name was Don Pedro Vázquez.''

Nicole immediately imagined Don Pedro as a tall man with dark hair and green eyes. ''He was handsome, I bet.''

Greg shrugged. ''I don't know. I never discovered a portrait of him. But I infer from his diaries and letters that women found him appealing.''

''Oh, I'm sure they couldn't resist him,'' Nicole murmured, taking in Greg's strong jawline and beautifully carved cheekbones. ''Go on.''

''The ship Don Pedro sailed on was headed for Mexico. This was about ten years after Cortés wiped out the Aztecs. Actually, he didn't do it by brute force alone. Smallpox killed off half the population of the Aztec empire within six months. They had no resistance to the virus. The streets of their capital, Tenochtitlán, become choked with bodies. This was a city which had never known an epidemic before the Spanish arrived.''

''Horrible,'' Nicole said. ''But don't forget that the Aztecs predicted their own doom at least a century before. That's another reason Cortés conquered them so easily, I believe. They were resigned to their fate.''

Greg looked a little chagrined. ''I forgot I was talking to a research anthropologist. Why did you let me rattle on about something you probably know more about than I do?''

Because I love the sound of your voice, Nicole answered silently. The very timbre of it pleased, soothed, delighted and thrilled her.

"I don't know a thing about Don Pedro," she said aloud. "Tell me more about him. You left him on a ship sailing to Mexico."

"He never made it. The ship got badly damaged during a storm and swept off course. It ended up in the vicinity of Saint Sophia, where it sank."

"And that's the ship you're looking for?"

Greg laughed ruefully. "If it were, I would have accomplished what I set out to do long ago. I found that wreck the first year I was here. Or at least the hill of ballast and enough artifacts to prove it was the ship Don Pedro was traveling on, which was called the Santa Ana. But there weren't any treasures on it. It was coming from Spain, don't forget. Finding it strengthened my belief in Don Pedro's diary reports, though. It made me more determined than ever to find the Buenaventura."

"I'm confused," Nicole said.

"And you're probably getting sleepy. I'll finish this bedtime story another time."

He started to get up but Nicole placed her hand on his shoulder. "Please don't go," she said.

He looked at her with both longing and restraint. "It's very late, Nickie."

"I don't care. You can't leave me hanging like this. I won't be able to sleep a wink unless I hear the end of your story."

"Is that the only reason you want me to stay?"

She shook her head slowly. "I'm not sure. All I know is that I don't want you to go."

His eyes caressed her face and bare shoulders, but he made no move to touch her. "I don't want to go, either." He leaned back across the width of the bed, propping himself on his elbows. "Well?" he asked softly. "Where do we go from here?"

Nicole settled back into the pillows. "Where did Don Pedro go once the ship sank? Not to his final reward, I hope."

"No, of course not. If that had happened, there would be no more story, and you and I wouldn't be in bed together on the island of Saint Sophia. For all I know, I'd still be teaching at Yale, married to Barbara, with two and a half kiddies by now."

Thank goodness Don Pedro hadn't drowned, Nicole thought. "So I gather he swam to shore," she said.

"He managed to, just barely. At that time Saint Sophia was occupied by Caribs. The chief's daughter, Lanalao, found him half-dead on the beach. She secretly nursed him back to health and then begged her father to spare him. She must have been a very persuasive young woman, because her father accepted Don Pedro as his son-in-law and gave a huge wedding feast. Normally, a stranger washed ashore would have *been* the feast. The Caribs were cannibals."

"Don Pedro must have been pretty persuasive himself to escape such a fate."

"I like to think that love saved him."

Nicole smiled. "You're an incurable romantic, Greg."

"They say it's a contagious condition." He took her hand and kissed the inside of her wrist, pressing his lips against her pulse.

"I've been inoculated," Nicole said, drawing back her hand. She could still feel the warm imprint of Greg's lips on her wrist and wondered what it would be like to feel that imprint all over her body. At the same time she reminded herself that only fools rushed into anything, and her cautious nature took control again. "Let's go back to the story of Don Pedro."

"If you insist."

"You started it. So now you have to finish it."

"Three years later a Spanish ship arrived and—"

"Wait a minute. What happened during those three years?"

"Don Pedro and Lanalao settled down to wedded bliss, of course."

"How do you know that?"

"Will you let me tell the story my way, please, Nicole?"

She bowed. "Proceed."

"Anyway, three years later a Spanish ship arrived," he began again. "And a large party of soldiers rowed to shore in search of fresh water. The Caribs didn't exactly welcome these invaders with open arms and a battle ensued. Half the tribe was killed. And Don Pedro was rescued. Actually he refused to leave Saint Sophia, and his rescuers had to hit him over the head and carry him off to the ship unconscious. They thought he'd gone mad. But the truth was he wanted to stay with his Carib wife and baby son. And *that*'s how I know they had settled down to wedded bliss."

Nicole sighed. "Did he ever see Lanalao again?"

"Don't jump ahead of the story," Greg told her. "The rescue ship brought him to Mexico. He recorded what he experienced there in some journals that I found in the Seville archives while I was doing my dissertation research."

"Funny that you should be a researcher, too," Nicole said. "When I met you at Jane's wedding I was sure we had absolutely nothing in common."

Greg reached over and brushed a golden strand of hair off her forehead. His touch made her scalp tingle. "We had a mutual attraction in common."

She glanced away. "I hadn't noticed."

"Hah! You certainly did. I saw the glint of desire in those cool gray eyes of yours, Ms. Webster. And if you'd dare look at me now, I would see it again."

She was sure he would, and rather than look at him, she took a great interest in examining her fingernails. "What did you discover in Don Pedro's journals, pray tell?"

"I wish I'd never mentioned him," Greg muttered.

Nicole gave his thigh a little nudge with her foot. "Come on. Tell me what you discovered," she prodded.

He released a deep dramatic sigh of resignation and continued. "Nothing new, really, although Don Pedro's firsthand account of the conquistador's ruthless search for gold was fascinating. He found their cruelty to the Indians intolerable and began protesting. A lot of good that did. He was sent back to Spain under armed guard. Apparently the king didn't want to hear Don Pedro's reports of injustices, either, because he banished him from court."

"Poor Don Pedro," Nicole said.

"Save your sympathy, sweetheart. He wasn't the type of guy to throw in the towel just because things weren't going well for him at the moment."

Nicole laughed. "You sound as if you knew him personally, Greg."

"I feel I did, in a way. When I read his journals I felt an immediate connection with him. His style would be considered a little stilted today, but I was amazed that he had such a progressive viewpoint. I wanted to learn all I could about him and eventually located some of his diaries. They were stored in a monastery outside Madrid, where he retreated after the king exiled him."

"Don Pedro became a monk?" Nicole couldn't picture him as one, perhaps because she pictured him looking exactly like Greg.

"No, he didn't become a monk," Greg said. "You see, he considered himself still married to Lanalao. In his diaries he wrote of his constant longing for his fierce Carib wife. The elegant, genteel Spanish ladies paled in comparison."

"She'd gotten in his blood," Nicole said, conjuring up an image of a wild, uninhibited woman of great passion. But an Indian woman wouldn't have had blond hair and gray eyes, would she? Feeling a little foolish, Nicole let this unlikely image of Don Pedro's Carib wife fade.

"Lanalao had gotten in Don Pedro's blood, his mind, his heart," Greg said. "Her name is on almost every page of his diaries. He somehow understood and accepted the savage part of her nature and it made him appreciate her gentler side even more. She had a great knowledge of herbal medicines, and he witnessed the almost miraculous way she nursed tribe members back to health. When Lanalao bore Don Pedro a son and he insisted that the boy be baptized with a Christian name, she'd agreed. The baby was named Miguel. Pedro often wrote about Miguel in his diaries, too. He worried that the boy would be lost to him forever and dreamed of bringing him and Lanalao back to Spain one day."

"Surely an impossible dream," Nicole said sadly.

"Dreams are impossible only if you give up on them, Nickie."

"You mean he actually managed to bring them back to Spain? But how could they function in such a formalized society? How could they be accepted? Maybe the boy could adjust, but poor Lanalao would have been a fish out of—"

"Stop jumping ahead of the story," Greg told her, squeezing her foot. "You haven't even come close to figuring out the ending."

Nicole shifted impatiently. "Now you've really got me curious."

"Just be patient. I certainly had to be while I was deciphering the old Spanish script of those diaries. Luckily I'd studied paleography and could manage it on my own."

Nicole nudged his thigh again. "Oh, stop bragging about how smart you are and get on with it, Greg."

"Sorry." He grinned. "Maybe I was trying to impress you just a little bit."

"You already did that long before now," Nicole told him. "And more than just a little bit."

"Oh, yeah?" Greg's grin widened. "And when exactly was it that I started making an impression on you, Nickie?"

"From the moment we met," she admitted. "You were right. There must have been a glimmer of desire in my eyes the day of Jane's wedding because frankly, Greg, I viewed you as a sex object. Sorry."

He waved away her apology. "Oh, that's all right," he assured her. "You have my permission to continue viewing me as one."

"Thank you." She contained a smile. "But we're getting off the subject again, aren't we?"

He gave her a blank look. "Which was?"

"Don Pedro's diaries."

Greg slid his hand up the blanket, molding the outline of her leg. "Who the heck is Don Pedro?"

"Your alter ego, I believe."

Her answer made Greg laugh. "I guess he is. He's certainly influenced my life for the past five years."

"Why?" Nicole asked. She leaned forward. "I still don't understand why you gave up everything and came to Saint Sophia, Greg."

"Sometimes I don't understand why myself," he replied dryly. "But here I am."

"Please don't be evasive," Nicole pleaded.

"I'm really not trying to be. But something very strange happened to me while I was examining Don Pedro's diaries in that musty monastery library. I connected with him totally when I read about his love for Lanalao and his son. He never mentioned them in his official journals. And then I came across another piece of information that he'd never mentioned in his journals. A shiver went up my spine when I realized I was the only one who knew about it. I could feel Don Pedro's presence in the room, urging me to *do* something about it."

Nicole felt a shiver herself. "Go on," she whispered.

"Before he got thrown out of Mexico for making trouble, Don Pedro befriended an old Indian guide

who had served Montezuma. He knew where some of
the royal treasures had been hidden from Cortés but
feared they would eventually be discovered. He offered to show Don Pedro the hiding place if he promised to protect the treasures from destruction.''

''And of course he agreed,'' Nicole said. She felt as
if she knew Pedro Vázquez almost as well as Greg did.

''You bet he did. He didn't want these priceless artifacts melted down. He valued the art more than the
gold. He described the treasures in his diary. Gold re-
ligious figures, gold and emerald ornaments, gilded
copper headdresses, hammered gold goblets and
plates, exquisitely designed jewelry.'' Greg took a
breath. ''The list goes on and on.''

''Why did he risk recording all this?''

''Because he was a dedicated historian, Nickie. He
felt compelled to leave a chronicle for future generations. He knew his diaries would be safe with the
monks when he went back to Mexico.''

''How did he manage that if he was in such disfa-
vor at court?''

''Politics and influence. Don Pedro was a wealthy
man, not without friends in high places, and he was
determined to return to the New World. He traveled
back to Mexico on the Buenaventura.''

''Aha! I was wondering when your mistress would
make an appearance.''

Greg laughed. ''She's been waiting on the sidelines
all this time. Just picture her, Nickie—with her bulky
wooden hulk of a body and three blowsy sails. She was
a creaking cargo ship, and six months after she anchored in Mexico she set sail for Spain again, filled to
capacity with—''

"Gold and silver," Nicole guessed.

"No, Nickie. Lumber. The timberlands were stripped along with the temples and mines during that time. There was nothing intriguing about the Buenaventura's cargo. Or at least there wouldn't have been if Don Pedro hadn't been traveling on her. It's a matter of record that he boarded that ship. It never reached Spain, though. That's also a matter of record. The Spanish kept very precise records." Greg smiled. "But there was something on the Buenaventura besides lumber, something that couldn't have been recorded on the manifesto because it had been smuggled aboard."

"The Aztec artifacts," Nicole said.

"That's right. Don Pedro vowed in his diaries that he would bring them back to Spain for safekeeping, relics of a destroyed civilization. Knowing what the Buenaventura's return cargo would be, he planned to hide the treasures in hollowed-out tree trunks."

"Do you have proof that he actually did that?"

"Sure I do." Greg shifted and dug into the pocket of his slacks. He tossed the gold seashell into Nicole's lap. "According to my pal Pedro's list, there are ninety-nine more of these. And they're somewhere on the bottom of the sea, along with all the other artifacts he listed. I discovered his diaries, and now it's up to me to discover his lost treasure."

Nicole stared down at the seashell and felt like weeping. Greg's quest seemed so hopeless to her. The Buenaventura could have been lost anywhere in the thousands of miles of water that separated Mexico and Spain.

"Hey, why such a long face, Nickie?" Greg tilted up her chin with his finger. "I'll find what I'm looking for because I know exactly what happened to the Buenaventura. It didn't sail directly back to Spain. Don Pedro bribed the captain to take a little detour to Saint Sophia so that he could pick up his wife Lanalao."

"That sounds too impossibly romantic, Greg."

His tanned, lean face took on a stubborn set. "Romantic, maybe. But not impossible. Don Pedro stated that he intended to do this in his diaries. Besides, island legend supports my theory."

Nicole sighed. "If there's one thing I know, Greg, it's that legends have only the smallest particle of truth in them. The rest is all invention and exaggeration."

"But there *is* a basis of truth in them," Greg insisted. "At least listen to this one before you debunk it, Nickie."

She reined in her skepticism. "Yes, of course I'll listen," she said. "With an open mind," she added.

"Good. Keep an open heart, too, okay, sweetheart?"

Didn't he realize that she'd opened her heart to him hours before? She nodded.

"This is a Carib tale," Greg began. "When I first came here I sought out an expert who related it to me."

"The Buenaventura is mentioned in Carib folklore?" Nicole became a little more optimistic.

"Not by that name. They call her Flaming Sails, the devil vessel that took the sorceress Lanalao's love away."

"Lanalao is part of the legend?"

"Yes. She was a tribal chief's daughter revered by the Caribs because of her magical healing powers. Sound familiar so far?"

"That fits Don Pedro's description of his wife in his diaries," Nicole conceded.

"Apparently Lanalao believed she had other powers, too. She was convinced that she could make the devil vessel that had taken away her husband bring him back again. She organized a group of followers who chanted for his return on the beach every sunset. They chanted for seven hundred sunsets and then, sure enough, they saw the three great sails appear on the horizon. Seven hundred sunsets, Nickie! That's about two years, which matches the dates between the time Don Pedro was abducted from Saint Sophia and then boarded the Buenaventura in Mexico."

Nicole arched an eyebrow. "Interesting coincidence."

"Coincidence, hell!" His green eyes gleamed with intensity as he stared at her. "Come on, Nickie. Admit it's more than that."

"It's eerie," she allowed.

"It's a retelling of what actually happened from a Carib's perspective. They lit big fires on the beach to draw the vessel to the island. Lanalao waited at the tide's edge, calling out her love's name over and over again, until he came ashore alone in a small boat."

"What name did she call out?" Nicole asked.

"The tellers of this tale didn't consider Pedro Vázquez's Spanish name important. They refer to him as the Man from Another Place. And you picked a fine time to interrupt again. I was just building up to the scene where Pedro and Lanalao reunite and violins swell in the background.''

Nicole laughed. ''Violins?''

''Okay, drums. Big, heavy drumbeat in the background. They embrace. The Caribs cheer. Or maybe bow down. Or maybe jump up and down. They did whatever Caribs at that time did to demonstrate their approval and happiness. They must have been amazed that Lanalao had managed to pull off this great feat. She'd vowed to bring her man back and dammit, she did!''

''What a gal,'' Nicole said archly.

''Yeah, Lanalao was quite a gal.'' Greg's tone became more serious. ''While she and Don Pedro were intimately celebrating their reunion that night, she ordered Carib warriors to row out to the anchored ship, sneak aboard and set fire to it. Hence the legend of the Flaming Sails.''

This turn of events stunned Nicole. ''What happened to all the Spanish sailors that were on board?''

''Most of them burned with the ship. Those who made it to shore were killed.''

''How could Lanalao have been so cruel?''

''The way she saw it, she was being expedient. The Spaniards were devil invaders to her and her people. The last time they'd paid a visit to Saint Sophia they'd killed off half the tribe. And stolen away her husband, the father of her child. She didn't want that to happen again, and who could blame her.''

''You're actually defending Lanalao!''

''She acted in keeping with her culture's beliefs and sense of justice, Nickie. I should think that as an anthropologist, you'd be able to understand that.''

"Intellectually I do. But it's hard to accept emotionally. What about Don Pedro? How could he have forgiven Lanalao for what she'd done?"

"Maybe he didn't know she was responsible. Or maybe he loved her so much that he found it in his heart to understand why she'd given that order. Maybe she really didn't, and the Carib warriors decided to burn the vessel on their own. As you pointed out, legends tend to romanticize history. And to the Saint Sophian Caribs, the Flaming Sails legend is a love story about Lanalao and the Man from Another Place." Greg paused. "Do you know what the Caribs on this island usually name their firstborn son to this day?"

Nicole clapped her hands. "Pedro!"

"No. Even better. They name him Miguel, as Lanalao named her firstborn son to please Don Pedro. Now why would they do that unless everything I've told you is actual fact? And please don't say it's just coincidence again. I realize Miguel is a common enough name, but the Caribs here never called any of their other children by Spanish names. Except their firstborn sons. I think Lanalao, who was revered by her people, must have started that tradition on Saint Sophia."

"Wow." Nicole leaned back against the pillows. "You've presented a good thesis, Greg. I'm beginning to believe that the Buenaventura was the Flaming Sails ship of the legend. It all fits. But..." She sighed deeply.

"No buts about it," Greg said with the supreme confidence that both irritated and delighted her. "I spent months researching this and putting all the pieces together. And nobody else has before me. In over four and a half centuries, I'm the first one to do it."

"But darling," Nicole said. Trying to be gentle, she was only dimly aware that she'd called him by an intimate sobriquet. "If the Buenaventura burned and sank off the coast of Saint Sophia—and you've convinced me that it did—then that would mean that all the Aztec artifacts Don Pedro smuggled aboard the galleon were destroyed. The conquistadors didn't melt them down. Lanalao inadvertently did!"

Greg laughed. "Wouldn't that have been ironic? The woman Don Pedro loved destroyed what he had tried so hard to save. But the ship's cargo was stored *below the waterline*, Nickie. When the burning ship went down, the treasures sank to the bottom of the sea. And that's where they still are, waiting for me to claim them for posterity."

Nicole picked up the gold shell he'd tossed into her lap. Was it just her imagination, or did it begin to glow brighter and brighter as she stared at it in her palm? She wrapped her fingers around it.

"I want to go diving for the Buenaventura with you, Greg. I want to help you find her. How long would it take you to teach me how to scuba dive?"

"Not long, since you already swim like a fish. But it's not fun and games, Nickie. It's exhausting drudgery."

She kept her fist clenched around the seashell. "I don't care. I like hard work. Please let me dive with you."

He remained silent a moment. "Actually I could use some help. Toby doesn't want to come out on the boat with me now that he's so wrapped up in Jane. Every time I take him away from her he makes me feel guilty about it.''

"Then take me,'' Nicole said. "Let me help you.''

He slowly stood up from the bed. "I'll sleep on it,'' he said, stretching his long frame and then heading for the door.

Nicole couldn't believe it. He was leaving her! "You forgot your seashell,'' she said in a disappointed little voice.

He turned back. "No, I didn't. It's yours now, Nickie. My gift to you for having faith in my quest.''

Tears sprang to Nicole's eyes. She knew he couldn't have given her a gift that meant more to him. And now she wanted to give him one in return. A gift to both of them, she thought. She placed the seashell on the night table. "Come back to bed with me,'' she said in a tremulous voice and moved over to make room for him.

Greg stared at her intently. "If I accept, neither of us will get much sleep tonight, sweetheart.''

"I know that,'' Nicole said, boldly meeting his eyes. "I want you to make love to me all night.''

Chapter Ten

Greg continued to stare without moving, wondering how he could possibly refuse her. She looked so lovely in the lamplight, so impossibly irresistible. Then why was he hesitating? Hadn't he wanted this to happen from the first moment he'd laid eyes on prim, cool Nicole Webster? Hadn't he wanted to break through her defenses and tear down her wall of reserve?

Well, he'd succeeded. There had been nothing prim about her invitation, and there was nothing cool about her demeanor now. Her fine-boned, delicate face glowed rosy; her gray eyes held promises that could melt any man's resolve to do the right thing. And the right thing, Greg knew, would be to leave immediately. He cared for Nickie too much now to risk hurting her. They had no future together. She had her work back in Boston. He had his mistress right here.

But Nickie knew that all ready. She knew that he would never leave Saint Sophia until he found the Buenaventura.

Then she wanted the same thing he did, Greg told himself. She wanted a romantic interlude—all the more poignant and passionate because it was temporary. What was wrong with that? He smiled softly as he moved toward her. He would do everything in his power to please her now. He would be gentle and good to her. No one would get hurt.

He sat on the bed again and took her into his arms. "Sweet Nickie," he whispered, pressing her against his chest and breathing in her unique, flowery scent.

He stroked her shoulders and back lightly, feeling the heat of her sunburn on his fingertips. He would have to take care about that, he thought. It occurred to him that there was another thing he must take care about. Even if it broke the mood for a moment.

"Are you protected, sweetheart?" he asked.

"Yes," she answered, pleased that he'd asked. Some men would have taken what they wanted first, and then asked that fearsome question.

"My sweet Nickie," he said again and sought her lips.

He kissed her tenderly but tentatively, a little awkwardly. Nicole drew away. "What's wrong, Greg? That's not how you've kissed me before."

"I know." He shook his head in puzzlement. "Before tonight I simply wanted you."

"And you don't want me now?" Her voice caught in her throat.

"More than ever." His eyes blazed like emeralds when he stared at her. "Maybe too much. I've never wanted a woman more. That's why I'm trying to hold back. I want our first time together to be so special, Nickie.''

But as touched as she was by his sudden reserve, Nickie didn't want him to hold back. She plunged her fingers into his thick hair and crushed her lips against his. The kiss she gave him wasn't the least bit tentative. Or that tender, either. She kissed him with bold passion and the image of Lanalao kissing Don Pedro flashed into her mind. She wanted to be as uninhibited as that fierce Carib woman, if only for one night. She wanted to make love to Greg with wild abandon, as she'd never made love to a man before. He groaned as she deepened their kiss and she felt the power of Lanalao in her, the power all women had if they dared take it.

She drew back to let her man catch his breath and smiled at his dazed expression. Did he think she was so *sweet* now? She began to slowly unbutton his shirt, feeling the heat of his body, the rise and fall of his chest, and a mad impetuousness overcame her. She yanked open the shirt with one strong pull, tearing the buttons from the fabric. Shocked by what she'd done, she held her breath and waited for his reaction.

Greg looked astonished for a moment, and then a knowing smile stretched his lips. ''Why, you little savage,'' he muttered, pushing her down into the soft mattress. He tore off his shirt and the rest of his clothes and lay beside her on the bed.

She pressed and rubbed her body against his and slid her hands over his back and buttocks, glorying in the muscular strength of him. He moaned with pleasure and she delighted in her power to please him. "You're my slave now," she whispered.

Her breath was fiery against his ear and he could almost believe that this was true, that she had somehow enslaved him. He didn't care. He cared about nothing but having her and satisfying the most primitive of needs. He fumbled with the pink satin ribbons on the bodice of her white cotton nightgown, his mind numb, his fingers clumsy.

"Rip it off," she commanded.

He did, rending the fabric as easily as if it were tissue paper, then snapping the thin band of her panties to reveal her completely. Her body glowed in the lamplight, her breasts milky white with taut, pink buds, her limbs sleek and smooth and soft, the triangle of her maidenhead golden and lush. She took his breath away.

She lay back, still now except for the pounding of her pulses, and let him worship her with his eyes, his hands, his mouth. As he caressed and explored every inch of her, she became dimly aware through the haze of pleasure that she had somehow relinquished her control over him. Her slave had become her master. She didn't mind a bit. They were enacting a drama as old as humanity, the give-and-take, the back and forth of making love. As his fingers dipped into her most private femaleness, she gasped and gazed up at him.

Her pupils, he noticed, had dilated, darkening her silvery-gray irises to a deeper, stormier shade. There was a wildness in her eyes that he'd never seen before, never imagined. It both thrilled and frightened him a little. He felt as if her eyes were pulling him through time and space, to the beginning of time, before civ-

ilization, when there was only male and female and
that was all that mattered. She arched her slender body
like a bow, signaling that she was ready for him,
wanted him, needed him.

He slid into her so easily and became captured in her
soft chamber of love. He thrust deeper, more forcefully, to somehow maintain his power even as he lost
control. She was goddess and temptress, angel and
devil. She was Lanalao. She was Eve. She was the
woman of his and every man's dreams.

Nicole heard the thundering of Carib drums in her
ears, the mighty buildup of passion. She lost herself
in the rhythms of their ageless, pulsing dance of love,
digging her fingers into his sinewy back as the throbbing beat mounted within her. She cried out and
shuddered with pleasure as pure release flowed between them.

He held her tightly after they'd completed the
primitive rite of love, their passage into bonding inti-
macy. It was only then that he whispered her real
name, or at least the one she was known by in this
particular time and place.

When Nicole awoke, the first thing she did was
blush. And then she smiled and nestled her cheek
against her lover's back, breathing in his deliciously
masculine essence.

"Hello again," he said softly.

"How long have you been up?" she asked him.

"Just now," he said, turning around to gather her
into his arms.

She felt his hardness against her thigh. "In more
ways than one, so it seems."

"That's what you do to me, love. I warned you that we wouldn't get much sleep tonight." He captured her breast in his mouth and suckled.

She felt the pull of desire all over again. "I don't need much sleep," she assured him.

This time their lovemaking was more tender, more lighthearted, more playful. Greg discovered every place where Nicole was ticklish, and she learned that he adored having the small of his back massaged. They savored each other as if they had been created just to delight each other. Yet when they united, Nicole was overcome by the power of their passion once again. She lost herself in him, not knowing where her self ended and his began. So this is how it's meant to be, she thought.

Greg got out of bed and started dressing as the sun came up.

"Can't you stay a little longer?" Nicole asked him sleepily.

He smiled, zipping up his linen trousers, which were a mass of wrinkles after lying in a heap on the floor all night. Nicole had a strange, domestic desire to press them for him. She would have actually offered to if she'd packed an iron.

"You know what will happen again if I do, Nickie," he said.

She smiled back at him. "Yes, I know what will happen again. That's why I'm asking you to stay."

"You're an amazing woman, Ms. Webster."

She nodded, hugging a pillow to her naked breasts. "Compliment accepted and returned, Mr. Chase."

He picked up his shirt from the floor and shrugged into it. "Some wild creature tore this off me last night," he said.

Nicole laughed, embarrassed. "Sorry about that. I owe you a new one."

"I owe you a new nightgown."

They looked away from each other. In the light of day, an awkward silence descended upon them.

Greg spoke first. "Listen, Nickie, I want you to know that I don't usually rip nightgowns off women."

"And you think I make a habit of tearing men's shirts off?" Suddenly there was anger in her voice. Anger that he was leaving her. But what had she expected?

"No, I don't think you make a habit of it," he replied calmly.

She pushed back her mass of tangled hair, feeling disheveled and...wanton. "I want you to know something, too, Greg. Contrary to what you may have concluded from my behavior last night, I'm not a raving sex maniac."

He chuckled. "Normally I'm not, either. Something very strange and special happened between us last night, Nickie. Let's just leave it at that."

Leave it at that? Cold apprehension trickled through Nicole's veins. "You mean you don't want it to happen again?"

"I don't mean that at all!" He knelt by the bed and took her cold hand in his. He pressed it against his cheek. "You're a fantasy come true, sweetheart. You're the most beautiful, passionate woman I've ever made love to. I want what we have together to last as long as possible."

"As long as possible?" Nicole forced a laugh. "That sounds pretty temporary to me, Greg."

He looked at her, puzzled. "Well, you can't stay in Saint Sophia forever, can you?"

His practical question pulled her up short. What had she been thinking, anyway? The problem was that she hadn't been *thinking* at all. "No, of course not," she replied, keeping her voice steady and light. "I'm scheduled to go on a cross-country lecture tour starting February 10."

"That gives us three wonderful weeks, love. We'll cherish every day, each moment of them." He kissed her hand and rose from his knees. He seemed delighted with this time limit.

"Why are you leaving now?" she asked him. "It's so early."

"No, it's late for me. I go out with the fishermen every morning. If you want something good to eat tonight, I'd better catch it this morning."

"Well, good luck." Nicole didn't know what else to say.

He bent down and kissed her forehead. "You're wonderful. You make my heart sing, Nickie." After stating that in his low, quiet voice, he headed for the door and closed it softly behind him.

Left alone, Nicole exhaled a long, frustrated breath. What had she gone and done? She'd fallen in love with a footloose and fancy-free adventurer in little more than a week after meeting him, that was what! Stay calm and rational, she cautioned herself. Falling in love was a romantic fancy. What she'd shared with Greg was no more than a basic biological urge that she'd finally given in to. He was the one who'd tried to romanticize it, not she. *You make my heart sing, Nickie*. She laughed at his words. Since when did hearts sing? She laughed so hard that she almost started to cry. Taking from the night table the gold seashell he had given her, she rubbed it between her palms. That comforted her.

"What's wrong with Nicole Niece I wonder to ask," Marie said at lunch on the patio. "She's not eating up my famous callaloo soup, which I cook better than any other living soul on this island."

"Perhaps it's too spicy for her," Jane said. "Don't forget that Nicole is a New Englander, Marie. My brother raised her on a diet of brown bread, baked beans, and overcooked codfish and pot roast."

"The callaloo is delicious," Nicole said. She wrenched her mind off Greg and forced three spoonfuls of the soup into her mouth, one right after the other. It was spicy, all right. She reached for her water glass.

"How did you enjoy your visit to Soufrière this morning?" Marie asked her.

"I think Nicole was disappointed," her aunt answered for her as she gulped down water. "She pictured some fiery monster belching smoke and ash."

Marie laughed. "Perhaps I am to blame for such a picture. We islanders like to make Soufrière sound full of mystery and danger to our visitors from cold climates. We never mention that he smells like rotten egg, though."

"The smell of sulfur, actually," Nicole said. She hadn't much enjoyed wandering among the mud holes and sulfur pits of the volcano crater all morning, even though it had been a chance to be alone with her aunt. "It's hard to believe people used to bathe in the springs."

"Oh, they're very therapeutic," Jane assured her. "In fact, Toby had me soak my ankle in one right after I twisted it."

When she'd heard about the accident from Marie over the phone, Nicole had imagined her aunt almost falling into—being pushed into?—a wide, deep caldron, but Soufrière had turned out to be a caldera, a collapsed volcano formation.

"Where would you like me to take you this afternoon?" Jane asked her. "We could go to the dock and watch a banana boat come in. Or we could visit an old fort the Spanish and French used to constantly fight over."

Neither option seemed terribly exciting to Nicole. "Oh, I don't care," she replied.

"What's wrong, dear? You seem so... listless."

"Too much sun yesterday is my venture to guess," Marie said, shaking her finger at Nicole.

"No, I'm fine. Perfectly fine." She attempted a smile. "I just have a lot on my mind at the moment."

"You're supposed to leave your worries behind when you vacation in the Caribbean," Jane said.

The image of Greg pushed its way into Nicole's mind again. She couldn't stop thinking about him. "What I left behind was my common sense," she muttered.

"What did you say, dear?"

"Nothing, Jane." She stretched her false smile wider. "I think I'll spend the afternoon working, if you don't mind. I lugged all those research books down here and haven't so much as given them a glance. Besides, I don't want to keep you away from Toby."

Marie laughed. "There's no keeping the two of them away from each other, Nicole Niece."

"So I've noticed." Her smile became sincere. Now that she was convinced that Toby hadn't married Jane for her money, she found their absorption with each other heartwarming. She reached across the table and touched her aunt's arm. "You're very fortunate, Jane. You've found your life's mate."

"Yes," Jane said. "Before I met Toby, I thought my life was quite complete. I had no desire to find a mate to share the rest of it with me. But Toby not only shares my life, he amplifies it. The sun shines brighter when he's beside me, the birds sing more sweetly when he hears them with me."

"Oh, such pretty talk!" Marie clutched her hands to her breast. "It reminds of a time, so long ago, when I strolled under the palms with . . ."

Nicole, who normally would have been interested in hearing Marie's story, stopped listening. The sun seemed to shine brighter all of a sudden, the birds to sing more sweetly. Greg had walked onto the patio, dressed in his faded cutoff jeans and a pale blue T-shirt that molded his chest.

"Greetings, ladies," he said, looking only at Nicole.

"Big catch you left in my kitchen this morning, Greg Mister," Marie told him. "Since we have no guests to feed but Niece this evening, I shared the bounty with some friends and relations."

"Fine," Greg said abstractly. All his concentration was centered on Nicole. A little smile played on his lips.

"We visited Soufrière this morning," Jane told him.

"Fine," he said again, hooking his thumbs in the belt loops of his jeans as he stared at Nicole.

"And then the cow jumped over the moon," Jane added.

"That's nice." He shifted his weight from one leg to the other, his gaze beamed directly into Nicole's.

Jane and Marie started giggling, but Nicole remained still and quiet, as if hypnotized. She was vaguely aware of the conversation, of the laughter, but it seemed to come from another world. The only person who existed in *her* world at that moment was Greg. And she had an odd, dipping sensation in her stomach that her world had stopped turning on its axis.

"How would you like to start learning how to scuba dive now?" Greg asked her.

Nicole stood up instantly, hitting her thighs against the glass tabletop, causing the dishes on it to jiggle. "All right. Let's go."

"But what about your work, dear?" Jane asked.

"All those many books you brought down?" Marie reminded her.

She turned and looked at them blankly, as if she had no idea who they were and what on earth they were talking about. "Thank you for a lovely lunch," she said automatically as Greg took her hand and led her away.

* * *

"I don't want to do it," Nicole told Greg three days later. They were on his boat, an old wooden craft that had originally been a shrimper. Greg had rebuilt and rigged it to serve as a salvage vessel. They were about a hundred yards out to sea, completely alone.

"It's time you did," he insisted.

Nicole was near tears. How could this man, who had been so kind, so patient, so *loving* toward her these past few days, be so cruel and heartless now?

"Haven't I proven myself to you already?" she asked him, voice quavering.

He sighed. "I'm not asking you to prove anything to me, only to yourself, Nickie." He hugged her, then slid his hands along the bare expanse of flesh below and above the red strips of her bikini. "I certainly won't make you do anything you don't want to do. Ever."

"I know." She clung to him. "I'm sorry to disappoint you, Greg."

"You haven't." He patted her back reassuringly. "You had no qualms about doing it in the cove yesterday," he reminded her softly.

"But this is different! This is over my head! I still don't understand why it's necessary to do it under these conditions."

"Because these would be the real conditions, Nickie. You're never going to have to do a bailout while you're in shallow water. You'll be on a boat that's sinking or on fire."

"Or being attacked by pirates?"

"Anything's possible on the high seas," he replied, ignoring her sarcasm. "The point of this exercise is to give you total confidence underwater, so that you'll never panic if something goes wrong.''

"What if I panic now?''

"You won't. I'll be right there with you. Come on.'' He handed her a weight belt. "You can do it.''

Nicole hoped that he wasn't overestimating her abilities. He expected her to jump overboard hanging onto her gear, sink to the bottom, and then put on her equipment while submerged. It was the last test he wanted to submit her to before he took her diving for treasure.

She'd had no idea what she was getting herself into when she'd asked him to teach her how to dive. He'd been an exacting instructor, drilling her in techniques, safety procedures, even underwater communication signals. She couldn't let him down after all the hours he'd spent training her for this moment. She couldn't let herself down.

"Okay, I'll go for it,'' she said.

He smiled, pleased. "If you don't succeed the first time, don't worry about it,'' he told her, putting on his own diving gear. "We can try again tomorrow.''

"I'll do it right the first time,'' she said, wrapping the webbed nylon belt, decorated with three lead weights, around her slender waist. "You think I want to go through this again?'' She snapped the safety release buckle with a decisive click.

"That's the spirit, sweetheart.'' He gave her a deep, lingering kiss, then lowered his mask.

"How far is it to the bottom, anyway?'' she asked trying to sound casual.

"Twenty feet. Twenty-five at the most. Just relax and take a few deep breaths before you plunge in.'' He watched as she gathered up her equipment to make sure she didn't forget anything, then helped her onto the gunwale, where she perched and stared at the water below.

"I'll be waiting for you down there, sweetheart." Giving her a jaunty wave, Greg rolled backward and disappeared.

Clutching her gear to her chest, Nicole said a brief prayer and jumped in after him. She'd assumed that she would sink quickly with a forty-pound air tank in her arms, but it took longer than she expected to reach the bottom. It took forever. Stay calm, relax, stay calm, she repeated to herself as Greg had advised her to do. He waited for her, kneeling on the sandy floor, nodding encouragement. Nicole knelt beside him and moved with the slow motion of frustrating nightmares, first turning on the tank valve, then putting in her mouthpiece and breathing from the regulator.

Feeling more confident now that she had air, she put on her face mask and cleared it of water. Then she slipped her hands inside the tank harness straps and began pulling it over her head. Greg shook his head and she remembered that she hadn't taken off her weight belt. Stay calm, no problem, she told herself. She put down the tank and placed the belt over her knees as she knelt. She pulled the tank over her head again, checked that the straps were secure, replaced the belt around her waist, and slipped on her fins. Greg held up two fingers. Elated by her accomplishment, she returned the V-for-victory sign.

How wonderful it was, Nicole thought, to have these little moments of triumph in life. How proud she felt as she ascended to the surface, buoyant with success. And how happy she was to have Greg by her side, coming up with her, their air bubbles mingling. Having Greg by her side was the best part of all.

Nicole lay in a jute hammock tied between two palm trees as the sun set that evening. She'd mentioned to Greg in passing the day before that she'd always pictured herself lolling in a hammock when she imagined being on a Caribbean holiday, and he'd driven to town to get one for her. She felt flattered that he'd gone to such trouble and a little guilty that he had. Well, more flattered than guilty.

She half closed her eyes, deliciously tired from the exciting bailout dive and the exalting lovemaking she and Greg had shared to celebrate her success when they'd returned to the boat. Recalling the heady sensation of the boat rocking beneath them as they rocked together, Nicole released a long, satisfied sigh. She felt a light fluttering on her face and neck, as if it were raining...flowers. She opened her eyes and saw bright pink hibiscus blossoms scattered all over her white peasant dress and bare shoulders. Greg stood over her, showering her with them. He was wearing his loose buccaneer shirt, the one he'd worn when she'd spotted him from the seaplane and her heart had flip-flopped. She smiled languidly.

"What are you doing?" she asked him.

"Worshiping you."

Her smile faded because she sensed that he wasn't really joking. Oddly, tears sprang to her eyes. "You'd better be careful, Gregory Chase, or I'm going to..."

"What, sweetheart?"

Fall in love with him? Was that what she'd almost blurted out? Lord, yes! "I'm going to take you seriously," she finished lamely.

He tucked a hibiscus behind her ear. "I hope you do take me seriously, Nickie, because I'm pretty darn serious about you. I can't remember when I've enjoyed myself more with a woman."

Would he remember *her* after she'd left Saint Sophia? she wondered. She pushed that painful question out of her mind. She had promised herself to take each moment as it came, to relish it and not think about the future at all.

"You were terrific out at sea this afternoon," he told her.

His praise warmed her. She picked up a blossom and twirled it between her fingers. "Thanks to your training and encouragement," she said.

"Well, if you insist, I'll take some of the credit." He started to grin. "But you're a natural, sweetheart."

"I guess I did take to it like a duck to water, so to speak," she agreed. "Of course, I had to get over my initial reservations. I'm so thankful I finally took the plunge."

"So am I," he agreed enthusiastically.

"I couldn't have done it without you, Greg. I was a total novice before you introduced me to the sport. I never realized how exhilarating it could be. Now I can't wait until we do it again."

His grin stretched. "Neither can I, Nickie."

"I doubt I'll ever get enough of it while I'm here."

"I'll do my best to make sure you do," he promised her, trying for a moment to look solemn but ending up smiling all the more broadly from the effort.

"Will you take me again tomorrow?" she asked him pleadingly.

"Why wait until tomorrow, sweetheart? I'll be more than happy to take you tonight."

"Oh, I don't know if I'm ready for that."

He released a dramatic sigh. "That's too bad, because I certainly am."

"But you're a pro, Greg. You've no doubt done it thousands of times, in all sorts of conditions."

"You overestimate my expertise and experience, Nickie." He shrugged modestly. "But if you enjoyed it so much this afternoon, why not do it again tonight?"

Nicole hesitated. "Are you sure we should? I'm so new at all this and I thought night diving was a little dangerous."

"Diving?" He widened his eyes in a parody of amazement. "I've been talking about the other 'sport' we indulged in on the boat this afternoon."

She threw the flower she was holding at him. It bounced off the edge of his broad shoulder. I don't consider lovemaking a *sport*, mister."

The humor vanished from his eyes. "Neither do I, Nickie." He knelt beside the hammock and kissed her ear, pressing his nose into the hibiscus flower he'd tucked behind it. "Neither do I," he repeated before claiming her mouth with his.

"So there you are." A hearty male voice rang out in the descending twilight.

Like two startled teenagers, Greg and Nicole broke from their kiss.

"Oops!" Toby laughed awkwardly as he came toward them. "Didn't realize I was interrupting anything more than conversation. Sorry. Jane and I went looking for you two because dinner's ready."

Nicole smiled at him. She liked him now. She'd wanted to like him from the very beginning and now that she trusted him, she could. "No need to apologize about dinner, Toby," she said, swinging her long legs off the hammock. "I'm starving!"

"Did you find them, honey?" Jane called from a short distance away.

"They're here, bunny," he called back.

Nicole's aunt joined them a moment later. She linked arms with her niece. Toby took Jane's other arm, Greg threaded his fingers through Nicole's, and the two couples strolled back to the inn. Lanterns hung from the rafters of the porch glittered in the twilight, beckoning them, and Nicole had a heartwarming sensation that they were all going home together. She reminded herself that her home was Boston.

"Guess who called today to reserve a room for next week, Gregory?" Jane asked.

"The president of the United States? The queen of England? The king of rock and roll?"

"No, Susan Fitzwell," Jane announced. "She asked if there was a free bed available. I told her that you would call her back."

"That awful woman!" Nicole said, forgetting for a moment that she had once believed Susan Fitzwell's disparaging comments about Greg. "She should be banned from Saint Sophia forevermore."

Her vehemence seemed to amuse Greg because he smiled. "I would never turn down a lady in need of a bed," he said.

Chapter Eleven

Are you going to tell me why you're angry with me?"
Greg asked Nicole that night.

She didn't look at him, seemingly fascinated by the
way the ceiling fan billowed the filmy netting that
hung from the tops of the bedposts. "I'm not exactly
angry," she replied.

"Could have fooled me. You barely said a word to
me during dinner."

Although Nicole wouldn't have objected to being
cajoled out of her bad humor by his caresses, he made
no move to touch her. "I can't understand why you're
actually going to let Mrs. Fitzwell stay at the Sea Rover
again." She lowered her voice to mimic him. "I would
never turn down a lady in need of a bed!"

Greg chuckled. "She's going to be a paying guest,
Nickie, and I could use the money."

"Meaning that I'm not a paying guest?" Nicole sat up. "Do you think I intend to mooch off you because I'm Jane's relative?"

Greg stroked her rigid back. "Don't be silly. I would never take money from you."

"Why? Is it your policy to let the women you sleep with stay at the inn gratis?"

"Actually, I make it a policy *not* to sleep with the guests," he replied patiently. "Are you trying to demean what we have together, Nickie?"

Her shoulders sagged. It was the last thing she wanted to do. "I'm sorry. That was a dumb thing to say."

"Yes, it was. But I forgive you." He pulled her down to lie beside him again. "Let's not quarrel about something that doesn't matter, sweetheart." His voice was soft and soothing. "Our time together is too precious."

But that was what she really felt so upset about—their time together was so limited! Didn't he understand that? He's not a mind reader, Nicole told herself. If you want him to understand, you'll have to tell him. "I'm going to miss you when I go back to Boston," she began.

"Hush." He silenced her with a kiss. "Let's not think about that now. We've got days and days of sunshine and pleasure and adventure ahead of us."

He sounded like a travel brochure, Nicole thought. Yet his touch was so gentle, so persuasive as he stroked and fondled her that all her misgivings melted away. When he moved his big body above hers, she accepted him willingly, eagerly.

* * *

Nicole awoke in the middle of the night and disentangled herself from Greg's embrace without disturbing him. Wrapping a blanket around her naked body, she went out to the porch and stared up at the stars.

"What is happening to me?" she asked them.

The stars had no answers. She slumped on the steps and wept silently not knowing why or for how long. But then she felt Greg's presence behind her and wiped her eyes with the edge of the blanket, thankful it was too dark for him to see her tearstained face. Without a word he sat down on the step beside her. Because he was naked, too, she shared the blanket with him, wrapping them both in the light cocoon.

"Are you okay?" he asked her.

She nodded, afraid her voice would give her away.

"If you feel that strongly about it, I'll tell Suzie Fitzwell she can't stay at the inn next week."

She cleared her throat. "It's really none of my business."

"You think Suzie and I had an affair, don't you? That's what's bothering you so much."

"Well, didn't you?"

"No. We were only business partners for a very short time. It didn't work out because she never really believed in my search. I should have known better than to let her invest in it. I'll never make that mistake again."

Nicole rested her head against his shoulder. "Do you think she's coming to Saint Sophia to cause trouble?"

"Not at all. I think she feels bad about that article she wrote and wants to bury the hatchet, which is fine with me. I don't hold grudges. It's a waste of time and energy."

Nicole nuzzled closer to him. "I feel the same way. But it's so much easier to forgive people you don't care about. I had to grow up before I could forgive my mother."

"For what?"

"For being herself, I suppose. She follows her heart wherever it may lead her. She left my father and me when I was a kid and went off to Paris with a man named Pierre." Nicole laughed sadly. "It was springtime, of course."

"So your father raised you?"

"More or less," Nicole said. "I went to boarding schools and spent the summers with Jane in Vermont. When my mother was between marriages, I sometimes lived with her. But that was later, when I was a teenager." She sighed. "By then we had absolutely nothing in common. I'm much more like my father, more analytical than emotional."

"Is that right?" Greg wrapped his arm around her waist under the blanket. "And were those analytical tears you were shedding when I came out to the porch?"

Nicole blushed. "I'm afraid there was no logic to them at all." She laughed it off. "I must still be all wrought up about my successful bailout this afternoon."

"It would pain me to think that I'm somehow making you unhappy, sweetheart," Greg told her softly.

She believed he really meant that. "These last few days have been some of the happiest in my life," she replied.

"I'm glad." He kissed her cheek. "And tomorrow will be even better," he promised. "We're going to go hunting for treasure, diving buddy. You're ready for the big time."

She squeezed his thigh. "Wouldn't it be terrific if we found the Buenaventura *together*, Greg?"

"It could happen," he allowed. "I've narrowed down the possibilities and feel I'm getting very close."

She squeezed his thigh again. "I'm getting excited."

"That's good, sweetheart," he said, grabbing her hand. "Because you're sure getting me excited." He slid the blanket off his shoulders and spread it on the porch floor. "Lie down," he commanded.

She obeyed, shivering a little as the night breeze fluttered over her body. Shivering in anticipation, too.

"Look up at the stars," he told her. "I want there to be stars in your eyes when we make love."

She gazed at him instead and her light eyes sparkled like diamonds when he lowered his face to kiss her.

"Don't forget that you're taking me diving with you today," Nicole reminded Greg when he rose with the sun the next morning. She would have liked him to take her fishing with him, too, but sensed that none of the other fishermen would have appreciated her tagging along.

"Of course I won't forget," he said. "I promised you, didn't I? I'll be back around ten." He gave her a quick goodbye kiss.

Left alone, Nicole felt restless. She slipped on her robe and unpacked the books she'd brought with her. Because there wasn't a desk in the room, she returned to the bed to read and take notes. She couldn't concentrate, though, as the the sweet scent of night blooming jasmine drifted through the open window. Disgusted with her lack of discipline, she slammed shut the volume on her lap and threw it aside. Then she immediately forgave herself. She was on vacation, after all. People on vacation were allowed to relax. She quickly put on a pair of shorts and a tank top and went down to the beach.

As she strolled along the shore, Nicole tried to make sense of the turbulent state of her emotions. She'd never been temperamental, yet ever since she had come to Saint Sophia she'd had trouble controlling her moods. A lot of that could have to do with the sudden change in climate, she told herself. It was perfectly normal for her body to react to such a drastic difference in temperature. She couldn't discount the effect Greg had on her, either, she admitted. But that, too, had to do with physiology. They had a highly charged sexual attraction. She smiled. At least now she understood what *that* was all about.

She turned around and walked back to the inn, feeling clearheaded and in charge of herself again. What she'd needed was some time away from Greg to put their relationship back into perspective. Satisfied that she had, she climbed the path leading to the patio. Jane was there, eating breakfast alone.

Nicole greeted her and joined her at the table. "Where's Toby?" she asked.

"Out fishing with Gregory. I'm not sure when they'll be back."

"Greg told me around ten before he left this morning." Nicole bit her bottom lip after letting that slip out.

Jane seemed to have missed the implication. "Fresh tamarind juice," she said, pouring her niece a glass of it. "What are your plans for the day, dear?"

Nicole took a sip of the tart juice. "Greg and I are going diving."

"Haven't you rushed into this too quickly, Nicole? I'm sure you know what you're doing, but you can't disregard the risks involved."

"Oh, don't worry. Greg will take care of me. He'll be with me the whole time and won't let me do anything dangerous."

Jane sighed. "He's the risk I was referring to."

"I don't understand." Nicole tensed. "I thought you held him in high regard."

"I do! But falling head over heels in love with any man you've know for such a short time is risky."

Nicole forced a laugh. "You're one to talk! You married Toby after knowing him for only a short time."

"Yes, dear. We *married*. We both wanted a commitment. Do you think Gregory wants one?"

Nicole looked away from her aunt. "Greg and I are having a delightful time together, that's all." She kept her voice light. "And I haven't fallen head over heels. My feet are still planted firmly on the ground. He's my madcap adventure. Every woman deserves one in her life.''

"Except there's nothing the least bit madcap about you, Nicole. That's what worries me. You always take things so seriously.''

"I'm tired of being so serious. I can handle this, Jane. I'm keeping it in perspective. Don't forget, I'm not totally inexperienced when it comes to men.'' Nicole took another sip of the juice and it made her lips pucker. She set down the glass. "Miles made me realize that it's unwise to expect too much from them.''

"Well, you shouldn't have expected too much from *him*,'' Jane replied. "But Gregory is superior to Miles Avery in every way.''

Nicole shook her head, perplexed. "I don't understand what you're trying to tell me, Jane. First you sound as if you're warning me about Greg, and in the next breath you praise him.''

"I think he's special. And I think you are, too, dear. When you first came to Saint Sophia, I even considered playing matchmaker.'' Jane hesitated for a moment. "But I never considered the repercussions until I saw how deeply involved you two had suddenly become.''

Nicole shifted uneasily. "There won't be any repercussions. I'll leave Saint Sophia with a tan and some beautiful memories and pick up my life exactly where I left off.''

"Will you?'' Jane looked doubtful. "Some women can handle casual affairs and take them in stride. I've known you for all of your twenty-six years, Nicole, and I don't think you're one of them.''

"You forget how practical I am," Nicole replied. "How levelheaded. A part of me remains objective at all times. Greg and I have totally different life-styles and I realize that we have no future together. So I view this...affair we're having as a temporary condition."

"Lord!" Jane rolled her eyes to heaven. "She makes it sound like a scientific experiment!"

"In a way it is," Nicole blithely agreed. "Field research on modern-day courting and mating practices." She plucked up a slice of papaya and nibbled off a piece. She hoped Jane didn't notice what difficulty she had swallowing it down.

Jane apparently did. "Just don't bite off more than you can chew, dear," she said gently. Then she dropped the subject and slid a plate of toasted banana bread toward her niece. "Put some of Marie's marvelous guava jelly on it," she advised.

Nicole knew that was all the advice Jane intended to give her for the time being. They'd always been careful not to interfere in each other's lives, and that was one of the reasons they'd always gotten along so well. The irony of the situation didn't escape Nicole, though. Now that she was no longer concerned about her aunt losing her head over a man who might break her heart, Jane was concerned about *her* doing exactly that. Everything had turned upside down since she'd come to this island paradise. And everything would get right back to normal once she'd left it, Nicole told herself.

A short while later Nicole drifted through a magical underwater realm filled with glowing colors and fantastic shapes. She moved with the weightless grace she'd only thought possible in dreams. All she could hear was her own heartbeat and breathing. It had taken her a while to overcome her amazement that she could actually breathe in the water, but now she considered it natural.

She glided past a meadow of undulating grass, past a school of hundreds of tiny fish arrayed in silver sequences, past a rock formation decorated with delicate red plants. How silky they looked. She longed to touch them. But Greg had warned her to touch *nothing* until she knew what it was. She didn't know the names of anything down here in this newly discovered world. Her ignorance humbled her but took nothing away from her delight.

She somersaulted both back- and forward and discovered that she could balance herself on one hand pressed against the sandy bottom. Better yet, she could balance herself on one finger! She stopped her antics and explored some more. What were these tiny velvet plants carpeting a ledge she passed? Something swept over her like a billowing cloud. What was that? Jellyfish, she guessed. She became frightened as a huge, bloated orange thing glanced against her face mask and then realized that it was only a harmless, overgrown goldfish.

How nice that flowers grew on the ocean floor, she thought, passing an array of feathery peach and orange algae. She glided through another patch of sea grass and it tickled her bare flesh. The pleasurable sensation reminded her of Greg's tongue-flicking caresses and she began to tingle all over.

Greg! Where was he? Nicole looked around and couldn't spot him. She had drifted away from him, although he had drilled it into her that staying close together was the first rule of buddy diving. But she'd gotten carried away with the beauty of her surroundings and forgotten it.

She felt totally disoriented now, without him by her side. She had no idea how to find the boat on her own and almost panicked. She mentally repeated the chant he'd taught her. Stay calm. Relax. Stay calm. It had worked the day before, during her bailout dive. But he'd been with her then. Now she was completely alone. She began breathing too quickly, using up precious air. Stay calm. Relax. Stay calm. But she couldn't! She was lost without him.

At that moment she forgot all his careful instructions and began flailing her fins against the water, rising much too fast, she knew, but only caring about reaching the surface. She felt something latch onto her ankle, yanking her back. Good Lord, what was it? A barracuda? She looked down, horrified. And then sweet, pure relief encompassed her. Greg!

He kept a tight hold on her ankle and with his other hand gave the underwater hand-talk signal, flat palm facing down, which meant, "Easy, slow down."

She nodded to show she understood and he released her ankle. With his index finger and thumb he formed a circle asking, "Is everything okay?"

Nicole nodded again, her breathing normal.

Greg pointed to himself. "Follow me."

She did, gladly, promising herself never to lose sight of him again. When he pointed up to indicate that they were rising, she nodded once again, enthusiastically, and he wrapped his arm around her waist. They broke the surface together, and Nicole spit out her mouthpiece.

"Thank goodness you made an appearance when you did," she gasped, clutching him.

He pushed her away and raised his mask. His eyes were glittering green orbs of fury. "Climb on the boat, dammit," he commanded.

Nicole had a little trouble hauling herself up the skinny ladder with the heavy tank on her back, and he gave her rear end a rather ungentlemanly shove to help her on her way. When he joined her on deck he divested her of her tank in the same brusque manner. He took off his own equipment without speaking to her.

Then he began lecturing her in his low, quiet voice. A tremor of rage ran through it. "The one thing I do not need in my life is an unreliable diving buddy," he said. "I thought that I had trained you very carefully, Nicole. But you've disappointed me. Didn't I tell you, over and over again, that you should never rise to the surface too quickly?"

She nodded as if they were still underwater.

"And didn't I tell you to stick to me at all times?"

She pounded her heart with her fist. It wasn't a hand signal he'd taught her, but she hoped it demonstrated how sorry she was.

Perhaps it did, because his severe expression softened. "You became mesmerized, didn't you?"

She nodded, grateful that his tone had become less critical.

"That sometimes happens the first time you're under for any length of time. I should have kept a closer eye on you, sweetheart."

She moved her palm toward herself, back and forth from the wrist. It was the underwater signal, "Come here."

He responded to it. "At least you remember the hand signs," he said, putting his arms around her and hugging her wet, salty body against his. "Oh, my dear Nickie," he said, clutching her tightly.

She could feel his heart thud against her breast. She closed her eyes and pressed closer against him.

"I'll never risk putting you in danger again," he said.

She stiffened. "You mean you won't let me dive with you again?"

"*Never* again. When I looked around and noticed you were gone, my heart almost stopped. I'll let you come out with me, but from now on you stay on the boat, safe and sound. I'm not going to even let you get your feet wet."

That didn't sound very exciting to Nicole. "I don't want to stay on the boat while you have all the fun underwater. I want to help you in your search."

"See, that's the problem, Nickie. You think of my search as fun and games."

"No, I don't!" she protested. "I realize how important finding the Buenaventura is to you."

"Oh, yeah? So while I was diligently fanning the sand, what the hell were you doing, diving buddy? You were enrolling in a passing school of fish, that's what."

She could feel his anger building again and decided that remaining silent would be the wisest thing to do.

"You got carried away like a little kid in a toy store," Greg continued. "Well, listen up, sweetheart.

I have better things to do than baby-sit for you during a dive."

Nicole forgot about the wisest thing to do. "Don't talk to me as if I'm four years old, Greg. I can handle myself down there."

"She can handle herself down there," Greg repeated to the puffy clouds above as he paced the deck. "Sure she can. That's why she strayed away and then panicked."

"Greg, I would appreciate it if you addressed me personally," Nicole said.

"No, you wouldn't," he told her. "Because then I would tell you how disappointed in you I am."

"You already did," she reminded him. "But this was only my first day. I'll prove myself tomorrow."

"This was your last day," Greg corrected. "Sorry, Nickie, but I care too much about you to take you diving with me again. I can't concentrate on my work and you at the same time."

"Is that final?" she asked him.

"Of course it's final!" His low voice increased a few decibels. "How many times do you have to hear it before it sinks in, Nickie?"

But what he'd said had already sunk in—deep. Nicole smiled. He cared about her. She couldn't have been more thrilled if they had found treasure.

Nicole strolled the beach alone the next morning and took great pleasure in kicking up sand. But then she inadvertently sprayed some over a beached starfish and stopped short.

"Oops, sorry," she muttered. That wasn't good enough, she realized, remembering what Greg had done when he'd come across a stranded starfish. She picked it up and tossed it back into the sea. She felt a little better after accomplishing her good deed.

"So nice of you to follow our island tradition," a thin, reedy voice declared.

Nicole swiveled around. A small figure dressed in a flowing white caftan was carefully placing her tiny feet in the footsteps that Nicole had left behind. Nicole recognized her immediately. Anabella Roseau.

"I didn't realize *I* was being followed," she said.

Nicole's remark was met with harsh laughter. "Don't praise yourself. I have far better things to do than follow you."

"Then why are you so carefully matching your steps with mine?"

"Only because they are in my path. I've come to collect shells." The old Carib's slanting amber eyes seemed to bore into Nicole as she gave her a challenging stare.

"This is a private beach," Nicole told her, feeling uncomfortable.

"But of course I have permission from Greg Mister to come here any time I please to, fair one."

"Please call me Nicole."

The old lady nodded. The top of her head came no higher than Nicole's shoulder blade. "And please call me Madame Roseau."

Nicole realized that she was dealing with a master of one-upmanship. "Are you really a witch, Madame Roseau?"

"Yes, but my power is limited to those who believe in it. Do you, Nicole?"

"No, I'm sorry but I don't, Madame Roseau. I'm a pragmatist. Do you know what that means?"

"It means you're an American," the old lady replied.

Nicole smiled. "Yes, I am."

"Born and bred in Boston. Raised by your scientist father because your mother left you when you were too young to understand why," Anabella added.

Nicole stopped smiling. "Who told you that?"

"No one. I heard it in your footsteps."

"You heard it from Marie or Jane or Toby or Greg."

Anabella raised her frail shoulders. "Whatever. I know what I know. You're unhappy now, because Greg Mister won't take you diving again. You did your best to convince him last night but none of your female ploys worked."

Nicole blushed. "He told you this?"

Harsh laughter again erupted from the little body. "When could he tell me? You have been with him every minute until he went away on his boat. You shook your fist at him on the dock. Now how could I know this except through my powers? I wasn't there, was I?"

"Maybe you were," Nicole said. "I wasn't looking for you at the time, Madame Roseau. But I will be from now on."

"You'll never see me, though. We Caribs have learned how to make ourselves invisible."

"That's quite a feat." Nicole tried not to sound too incredulous. "I've never met a full-blooded Carib Indian before."

"I have both Spanish and French blood running through my veins, too. But I'm one of the last descendants of the fierce island warriors, and Lanalao's blood pumps my heart."

"Lanalao? Were you the one who told Greg about her?"

"I told him many things." She offered her gap-toothed smile. "And now allow me to tell your fortune, Nicole. I charge ten dollars, but for you only five."

Nicole knew a hustler when she came across one but she remained polite. "I'm sorry, Madame Roseau, but I don't have a cent on me."

"Your loss then. I only offer when the spirit is with me."

Nicole was sure that the spirit would move her again if she saw a profit in it. "You speak excellent English, Madame Roseau."

"As a child I was sent to a missionary school in Saint Lucia. That was almost a century ago."

Nicole's eyes widened. "How old are you?"

"What a rude question!"

"I beg your pardon." Nicole smiled. Irascible as she was, this old lady was rather sweet. "Why don't you come back to the inn with me? I'll get my wallet and you can tell me my fortune." On impulse she took the old woman's arm.

The little Carib shrank back. "Never touch me without permission, fair one!"

Realizing that she'd committed a faux pas, Nicole began to apologize. But Madame Roseau stomped off, covering her ears with her hands.

"And then, when I tried to apologize, she put her hands over her ears and walked away." Nicole laughed nervously as she recounted the incident over dinner that night on the patio. She was trying to make light of it, but it had bothered her all day. The last thing she'd intended to do was offend Madame Roseau.

Suddenly all the candles in the hurricane lamps went out. A hush fell over the table. Marie made a quick sign of the cross. Toby grabbed Jane's hand. Greg smiled at Nicole and broke the silence.

"You should never have taken the liberty of touching her, but that's okay, sweetheart. You meant well and I don't think Madame Roseau will be vengeful."

"Vengeful?" Nicole frowned, feeling the tension in the air. "What are you talking about, Greg? She's a harmless old fraud."

"I am leaving this very moment," Marie announced. "To see to dessert, of course," she added as she hurried off to the kitchen.

"I'd better get some matches to relight the candles," Toby said. "Come and help me find them, Janey."

"They're in the first drawer of the—"

"Come with me, Jane," her husband interrupted.

"Well, if you insist, honey." She left the table with Toby.

"Since when did Toby get so demanding?" Nicole asked Greg.

"He's not taking any chances about Jane's welfare," he replied. "Sitting here with you could be dangerous right now. Madame Roseau may decide to send a bolt of lightning your way."

"Don't be ridiculous, Greg. That old lady has about as much power as—"

Crack! A fork of lightning branded the dark sky.

Greg grinned and leaned back in his chair. "Maybe you should try to get on her good side again."

"I'm not going to fall for your teasing," Nicole told him. "We all knew a thunderstorm was coming, and that's the only reason everybody rushed off. They could feel the electricity in the air."

Raindrops began to plop onto the glass table. Greg continued to grin. "Admit it, Nickie. You're more than a little bit inclined to believe in Anabella now."

"Absolutely not. And if she's the island expert you sought out to confirm your theory about the Buenaventura, I have second thoughts about accepting the legend of the Flaming Sails."

"Oh, you're just miffed because I wouldn't take you diving with me today."

"One thing has nothing to do with the other, Greg. But I *am* still angry with you about that."

"You could have come on the boat with me. I would have much preferred taking you instead of Toby."

"I didn't want to go along for the ride. I wanted to dive."

"You're stubborn," he said. The rain began to fall a little harder.

"No, you are." She crossed her arms. She wasn't going to leave the table until he did. How could he possibly accuse her of being stubborn?

He raised his face to the rain. "That feels wonderful," he said. "I bet you've never in your life run naked in the rain, Nickie."

"People don't usually go around doing that in Boston."

"You're not in Boston now, love."

She smiled. It was impossible to stay angry with him. Besides, she'd missed him all day.

He stood up and offered her his hand. "Let's go down to the beach. We'll have it all to ourselves."

"I've never made love in the rain, either," she told him, taking his hand. "I thought I'd mention that, for what it's worth."

"Oh, it was definitely worth mentioning," he assured her.

They ran down the path to the deserted beach, laughing like children. But when they reached the shore they became serious and quiet as they undressed each other, peeling off soaking garments and letting them fall to the sand. Lightning flashed across the night sky again and Nicole trembled a little. Greg enfolded her in his arms and soothed her, stroking her slippery body and warming it with kisses.

"Yes, it does feel wonderful," she agreed in a murmur but she wasn't talking about the rain.

The made love in the damp sand, gently, slowly, as the incoming tide licked at their toes. The raindrops spattered against Greg's broad back and Nicole's face. She opened her mouth to let them trickle down her throat as Greg moved inside her. While his body was hot and hard, the raindrops and sand were cool and soft, and she found the contrast of sensations delicious. He took his time with her, and she began to writhe and arch her back as the sweet pleasure mounted. Still he stroked her slowly and his determination not to rush eventually mastered her impatience. She moaned and melted and languorously moved with him. Their release came with a clap of thunder and Nicole laughed and cried as the pleasure exploded within her.

"How could you have timed it so perfectly?" she asked him after she'd caught her breath and could speak again.

"I can't take credit for the sound effects, love." He kissed her smiling lips and rolled his weight off her. Lying on his back, he looked up at the stormy sky as the rain poured down. "You're going to exhaust me yet, Nickie. Right now I feel like a beached starfish."

Her laughter was throaty and unsympathetic. Their lovemaking had invigorated her. "Then I'll have to toss you back into the sea."

She leaped up and grabbed his hands, trying to tug him up. He allowed her to, but once he was on his feet he lifted her up and cradled her in his arms. "Looks like the tosser has become the tossee. Don't you remember how easily I can do this to you?"

She remembered every detail of their every moment together and knew she always would. How warm and bright these memories would be on cold, lonely nights. But she wouldn't let herself think about that now. Instead, she kicked and wriggled in his arms, pretending indignant dismay. "Don't you dare throw me in the water," she said. "You'll get me all wet."

They both found this enormously funny as he plunged with her into the sea. The water was warmer than the rain. After swimming lazily for a while, they treaded water and kissed.

"Greg, will you take me—?"

"Yes! I give in. I'll take you diving with me tomorrow, if you promise to stay close to me."

"Great!" She wrapped her arms around him in a show of enthusiasm and they almost went under. She released him and resumed treading. "But what I had started to ask you was if you'd take me to see Madame Roseau."

"Why, if you think she's such a phony?"

"Maybe I was too quick to judge. I'd like to hear some of her old Carib tales."

"All right. We'll go visit her tomorrow when I come back from fishing." Greg turned his face up to the sky. "If that's okay with you, Anabella, give us a sign."

Nicole was actually disappointed when no flash of lightning followed.

"She must be asleep," Greg explained with a perfectly straight face. The rain ceased a moment later.

Chapter Twelve

Late the next sunny morning, sitting beside Greg as
he swerved his Jeep around a curve in the mountain
road, Nicole had misgivings about visiting Anabella.

"Madame Roseau may not appreciate us barging in
on her," she said to Greg. "Perhaps you should have
called first to let her know we were coming."

"Anabella doesn't have a telephone, sweetheart.
She doesn't need one. She always knows when visitors are coming." In fact he'd earlier sent a message to
her via one of the fishermen.

"You don't believe in her, do you, Greg?"

"I believe in her Carib legends," he replied. "The
rest . . ." He shrugged.

"I wish I had a tape machine to record her stories."
Nicole checked her canvas purse to make sure she'd
brought her notebook.

"She would never have allowed you to record her voice, Nickie. She's superstitious about things like that. Once someone tried to take her picture and she hit him on the head with his camera."

"Who was it? A tourist?"

Greg brushed his thick hair from his temple. "See that scar?"

"You?" Nicole almost laughed at the image of Greg getting bashed on the head by such a tiny old lady, but her concern that he'd been injured dimmed the humor of the situation. She leaned closer to examine his temple. "I don't see any scar."

"Really? I guess it must have faded after Anabella put some of her magical ointment on it."

Nicole slapped his arm. "You tease! She never hit you on the head at all."

"Well, maybe I exaggerated a little bit. She threatened to, though."

He took a sharp turn and the Jeep bumped along a rutted road so narrow that the overgrown foliage scraped against the sides of the car. He stopped in front of a dilapidated wooden cottage that seemed to grow out of the tangle of tropical vegetation. A large palm tree had toppled over and fallen onto the corrugated tin roof.

"Here we are," he announced.

"Do I look all right?" Nicole asked, tucking her sleeveless beige blouse into her khaki shorts. "Maybe I should have worn something more formal."

Greg's gaze lingered on her long, bare legs for a moment. "You look fine," he said. "Anabella doesn't care how people dress, but she does care about formality. Remember to address her as Madame Roseau until she gives you permission to do otherwise."

"Oh, I will. And I certainly won't touch her again!" Nicole alighted from the Jeep.

"Oh, and another thing, Nickie. Until you reach her porch, watch out for Anabella's pet snakes."

"Very funny," she said. Even though she was quite sure Greg was joking, she decided not to take any chances and ran to the porch, taking the sagging steps leading up to it two at a time.

"Who goes there?" a thin, reedy voice inquired.

Nicole looked around but there was no one in sight. Suddenly there was a fluttering, and the flash of a sharp pointed beak lashed close to her eyes. Nicole let out a startled scream and dropped her purse to cover her eyes with both hands.

"Don't be afraid," Greg said, running up the steps. He wrapped his arm around Nicole, and she leaned against him gratefully, still keeping her hands over her eyes. "It was only a parrot, sweetheart," he said. "And it flew away."

"It might come back."

"Let's go inside."

Nicole let him guide her over the threshold, and when she lowered her hands, she saw Anabella ensconced in a rattan rocker behind a low table.

"Why does your lady friend look so startled, Greg Mister?"

"Your stupid attack parrot frightened her, *Madam*."

"Diablo is not a stupid bird. He does my bidding."

"You mean you commanded him to attack me?" Nicole asked. She found it eerie that the parrot and the old lady sounded exactly alike. Assuming it had been the parrot who had asked, "Who goes there?"

Without replying, Anabella poured a cup of tea from a chipped enamel pot and offered the cup to Nicole. Greg gave her a little nudge and she stepped forward to accept. The cup and saucer tinkled in her shaky hand.

"I apologize for Diablo," Anabella said, then chortled. "But his beak is worse than his bite."

Nicole did her best to remain polite. "I hope we're not imposing. I told Greg that you might not appreciate us dropping in unexpectedly."

"Of course I expected you. I made you tea, didn't I? Sit down." It was more a command than a request.

Nicole glanced around the room. There were cracks between the wavy floorboards, and pages torn from catalogs and magazines covered the walls, a display of modern luxury items that contrasted sharply with the humble room they papered. The furnishings were meager—a table with rusting metal legs, a moldy chest in one corner, a few rickety, handmade chairs. She selected the one that looked the most stable.

"You sit too, Greg Mister."

"No thanks, *madame*. While I'm here I'd like to move that palm tree off your roof before it does any more damage."

"That would be appreciated, since I haven't the strength to do it myself," the old lady said.

Why doesn't she just use her magical powers? Nicole thought sardonically. But she was pleased that Greg had offered his help, even if it meant spending time alone with Anabella. The old lady with the parrot voice and shrewd, amber eyes made her feel more uncomfortable than ever.

After Greg had left them, they sat in silence and listened to him scramble around the tin roof.

"You hate losing sight of him for even a few moments, don't you, Nicole?"

"Yes," she admitted. "I do."

Anabella nodded. "Well, a pleasing enough sight he is. But you'll only be seeing him in your dreams when you return to Boston."

Nicole didn't want to be reminded of their temporary relationship and changed the subject. "Greg told me that you wouldn't let him photograph you. Why is that?"

"Good business."

"I beg your pardon?" It was hardly the answer Nicole had expected. "You're not afraid of the camera stealing your soul?"

"Such nonsense! I want Greg Mister to tell his tourist guests how difficult it is to take pictures of me. That way they will be eager to offer me money for the rare privilege."

Nicole narrowed her eyes. "Why are you letting me in on your little ruse, Madame Roseau?"

"It amuses me to," she replied. "You amuse me greatly, Nicole Webster." She poured a cup of tea for herself. "This is a special mixture of herbs that I blended with you in mind. But I notice you haven't sipped it yet."

Nicole looked down at her cup. She didn't have the slightest inclination to drink the pale golden liquid. Tiny twigs floated in it.

Anabella raised her cup to her lips and drained it. "There, you see. Perfectly harmless."

"I didn't think you were trying to poison me, *madame*." Nicole gulped down the herbal mixture. It had no taste whatsoever. "Very refreshing," she said.

"Why don't you take out your notebook and pen and begin recording my history?" the old lady suggested.

Nicole didn't even bother to ask Anabella how she knew that she intended to interview her or that there was a notebook in her purse. She looked around for it.

"You dropped it on the porch when Diablo greeted you," Anabella told her.

"If I go out to get it, will he *greet* me again?"

"No. Greg has no doubt disturbed him from his perch on the roof."

Nicole went outside and looked up at Greg. He'd taken off his shirt, and the muscles in his brown back rippled as he pushed at the fallen palm tree. The sight brought a dreamy smile to her lips. "Need any help?" she called up to him.

He stopped shoving and smiled down at her, legs spread wide to keep his balance on the slanting roof, hands on his hips. Against the backdrop of blue sky and palm fronds, he looked a hundred feet tall to her.

"No, I'm managing fine," he said. "But what about you, sweetheart? Need any help dealing with Anabella?"

"She finds me amusing. I haven't dared asked her why yet. How long are you going to stay up there?"

"A little longer. I might as well patch up the roof while I'm at it. Luckily I brought along my toolbox.

It seems something always needs fixing when I come here.''

"You're a very nice man, Gregory Chase."

"Well, it took you long enough to realize that," he replied gruffly and went back to shoving at the tree.

Even his grunts delighted her. Nicole could have stood there and watched him for hours, but then she remembered that Anabella was waiting for her. She retrieved her purse and went back inside.

"Are you directly related to Lanalao?" she asked the old woman, opening her notebook and uncapping her pen.

"Yes. That's why I have such powers. Only females can inherit Lanalao's powers."

"And who will inherit them from you?"

"No one. It ends with me. I have no children." She exhaled a long breath. "It doesn't matter. Too few believe anymore. But I want Greg Mister to find that ship. It will keep the legend of Lanalao alive."

"Will you tell it to me, please?"

"Gladly. But you've already heard it from him, haven't you?"

"I'd like to hear it in your words."

Anabella closed her eyes and began rocking slowly as she recounted the tale in her harsh, flat voice. Nicole took notes. It was the same story Greg had told her, but with more embellishments. Nicole, a stickler for details, appreciated them. As Anabella recited, Greg pounded at the roof, and Nicole imagined the sound as a Carib drumbeat in the background. And then there was only the drumbeat. Madame Roseau had fallen silent.

Nicole closed her notebook. "It's a fascinating legend," she told the old lady.

"But do you believe it?"

"I believe that the Man from Another Place was Pedro Vázquez, and that the Flaming Sail was the Buenaventura."

"Ah, so you view it differently than I. You don't believe that Lanalao had powers to bring her lover back to her."

"Yes, I do," Nicole replied softly. "She had the power of love to draw him back. Perhaps that's really the point of the legend."

Anabella continued rocking. "You will need great powers yourself to draw Greg Mister away from this island," she said. "He's determined to stay until he finds his sunken treasure."

"I realize that." Nicole's voice trembled only slightly. "I would never try to make him leave."

"That is wise," Anabella said. "But I cannot foresee him finding his ship for many years to come."

"How many?" Nicole couldn't help but ask.

"When I see the future, time has no exact measurement."

"What else do you see?"

Anabella stretched her thin lips into a smile. "Such eagerness in your eyes to know. I thought you had no faith in my abilities."

Nicole shifted uncomfortably and said nothing.

"Your longing overcomes your doubts, though," Anabella continued. "You long for your time with Greg Mister to last forever. But you will be leaving Saint Sophia alone, Nicole. He will not be accompanying you."

"I never expected him to."

"But what we expect and what we desire are two different things, are they not? What I find so very amusing about you, fair one, is your determination to keep a cool head as your heart burns with passion."

"Yes, I am determined to do that," Nicole said, not finding it the least bit amusing.

Anabella laughed and laughed as she rocked back and forth. She stopped and gave Nicole a piercing look. "Do not dismay. Your man will find the treasure he is seeking. It won't be the one he's been looking for, though."

"But didn't you just predict that he'll eventually find the Buenaventura?"

"That, too. But that will happen much later."

"You speak in riddles, Madame Roseau. It's very frustrating."

Compassion flickered in Anabella's bright eyes. "Poor Nicole. How unhappy you will be when you leave this island."

Nicole waited for her to go on but she said nothing more. "That's it, *madame*? That's all you're going to tell me?"

The old woman winked. "What do you expect for five dollars?"

Nicole reached for her purse to cover up her disappointment. For a moment there she'd actually believed in Anabella's powers. Now she felt foolish. She took a five-dollar bill from her wallet, sure that what she'd just heard wasn't worth five cents. But a deal was a deal. "Will you accept American money?" she asked coolly.

Anabella shook her head.

"But the exchange rate would be favorable to you."

"Give me a personal possession of yours instead," Anabella demanded. "One that you've often handled. A piece of jewelry, perhaps."

"I'm not wearing any," Nicole said, thankful she wasn't. She had the feeling that this clever old fraud could trick her into turning over the Hope diamond.

"A tube of lipstick, then," Anabella suggested. "A powder compact."

"I don't have any makeup with me." What on earth did this woman really want? she wondered.

"Very well. Give me your pen."

"But it's just a cheap one," Nicole felt obliged to point out. "I don't think I paid more than a dollar for it."

"That's what I want as my payment for telling your fortune," Anabella insisted.

"Very well." Nicole handed it to her. Why argue?

Anabella beamed her gap-toothed smile. "How nice of you to humor an old lady, Nicole. You won't regret it."

She tucked the pen into the pocket of her caftan, got up from her rocking chair and went across the room to the old chest in the corner. She stooped and at first Nicole thought she heard the old Carib's bones creaking. But it was the sound of hinges as Anabella opened the chest.

"Come here, Nicole. Come see my relics from the past."

Nicole obeyed and knelt beside her to examine the chest's contents, breathing in a musty smell. "Oh, what's this?" she asked, about to reach for a silver medallion resting on a bed of dusty purple velvet. She thought better of it and drew back her hand. "May I touch it?" she asked.

Anabella gave her permission with a sharp nod.

"It's beautiful," Nicole said, examining the intricately designed piece of silver depicting a cross entwined with roses.

"It was Don Pedro's," Greg's voice declared from the doorway.

"No, it can't be." Nicole looked up from the medallion and watched him walk across the room, his shirt slung over his shoulder, his chest gleaming with sweat from his work on the hot roof. She imagined the medallion hanging from a chain around his neck, swaying against his bare skin as he moved.

"Of course it could be his," Greg told her. "It's definitely a Spanish design from the sixteenth century."

"Did Don Pedro ever mention wearing a medallion in his diaries?"

"No, why would he?" Greg asked impatiently. He made his voice high. "Dear diary, today I'm going to wear my silver medallion with the cross and roses."

Nicole ignored his ridicule. "It would have verified the provenance if he had, Greg. Now it's just wishful thinking."

"*I* verify it," Anabella declared majestically. "This medallion has been passed down to Lanalao's descendants for over four hundred years. The Man from Another Place was wearing it around his neck when Lanalao found him washed up on the beach and brought him back to life."

Nicole traced the engraved silver with her finger, just as she pictured the fierce young Carib doing the

first time she saw it. And then she pictured Lanalao
sliding her hand over Don Pedro's chest as he lay unconscious, tracing the muscles. Love at first sight? The
stuff of romantic legends, she thought.

"Please show Nicole the map, *madame*," Greg said.

Anabella carefully picked up a rolled parchment
and even more carefully unfurled it. Nicole looked
over her shoulder at a rough outline of Saint Sophia.

"I keep telling Anabella that such an ancient map
belongs in library archives, not her old trunk," Greg
grumbled. "So does the medallion. They're priceless."

"They're *mine*," the old Carib corrected. "This
map was drawn by another relative of mine, an early
French settler who married Lanalao's granddaughter.
It depicts Carib villages around the island that the
settlers were wise to avoid." She pointed to the faded
brown *x*'s with her gnarled finger. "We still ate island
invaders in those days," she added in a matter-of-fact
tone.

"Not very good for the tourist trade," Greg remarked dryly, kneeling behind Nicole. She could feel
the heat of him through her thin blouse.

"Alas, the villages were destroyed and the Caribs
who lived in them slaughtered centuries ago," Anabella said. "The tourists who come to your inn are
quite safe, Greg Mister. I happen to be a vegetarian."
She rolled up the parchment.

"Anabella let me make a copy of the map," Greg
told Nicole. "I figure that the Buenaventura must have
gone down less than a mile off one of those sites, since
the villagers could see it burning. But which one? I've
explored the waters around twelve of them so far."

"There were at last twenty x's on the map," Nicole said.

"Twenty-three." She felt Greg's chest expand and then felt his warm breath on her neck as he sighed. "And who knows if any of them mark Lanalao's village? If only Don Pedro had drawn a map in his diaries. But that would make it too easy for me." Greg stood up and stretched. He helped Anabella to her feet and then Nicole.

"I will put the gift you gave me in my trunk," the old woman told Nicole. She extracted the pen from her pocket. "Make a wish before I do."

Nicole's thoughts immediately went to Greg. She wished that he would discover his treasure and find peace and contentment.

"He will," Anabella said, as if Nicole had voiced her wish. She threw the pen into the trunk and slammed the lid shut.

"What was that all about?" Greg asked.

Rather than answer him, Anabella insisted that he have a cup of her herbal tea before leaving. And that Nicole have a second one. Their hostess eased her frail little body into the rocking chair and picked up her chipped teapot.

Sure that none of the rickety chairs in the room could support a big man's weight, Greg chose to sit on the floor beside Nicole and balanced the little cup and saucer Anabella gave him on his knee.

"This tea is very medicinal," she said, handing Nicole a refill. "It cures whatever ails you."

Spoken like a true snake oil salesman, Nicole thought, and raised the cup to her lips to cover up her smile. She'd felt no ill effects from her first dose of the beverage and didn't think a second would do her any harm.

"How do things go at the Sea Rover?" Anabella asked Greg with a tea-party politeness. "Your cousin is well, I hope."

"Toby has never been better," Greg replied. "And never happier."

"But of course he's happy, married to the Bird Lady. I predicted that she and Toby Mister would end up in marital bliss the first day she arrived on Saint Sophia, didn't I?"

"Yes, you did," Greg said. "You stated it right in front of her whole Audubon group and embarrassed Jane and Toby completely."

"Well, she asked me what was in her future, and so I told her directly."

Nicole found herself wishing that Madame Roseau had been more direct in predicting *her* future instead of talking in riddles. Then she remembered that she didn't believe in the old Carib's powers.

"So Madame Breck is going to purchase land on the leeward coast for a bird sanctuary," Anabella said. "I approve."

"How did you know about that?" Greg asked.

"I would like to claim I saw it in a vision, but in truth I know through rumors. By now you must realize that everyone knows everyone else's business here, Greg Mister."

"Well, I hope the European hotel chain buying up prime property around here doesn't get wind of it. They might start bidding for the same tract of land."

"Not to worry," Anabella told him. "The land will be Madame Breck's soon, and she and your cousin and the birds will be happy."

Pleased with her prediction, Greg thanked her for the tea and stood up. Nicole rose, too, and offered her hand to Anabella, not sure if she would take it or not. Shaking hands, after all, involved touching.

But the old woman not only took Nicole's hand— she clutched it firmly. Nicole had the image of a bird claw twining around her fingers.

"It's too late to prevent what will happen in the future," Anabella told her in parting.

Nicole extracted her hand from the fierce grip. "Not very comforting words, Madame Roseau."

"You may interpret them any way you choose."

Greg chuckled. "She's playing mind games with you, Nickie."

Anabella's slanting bright eyes took on a blank look. "What games are those?"

"The ones you are a master of, *madame*. I hope you haven't said anything to upset Nicole today."

"Have I?" Anabella smiled at her, baring her long, yellow teeth.

"I'm not sure," Nicole replied. "I need time to think about it."

"You think too much," the old Carib told her.

Chapter Thirteen

The days were blending one into the other for Nicole, and she began to understand what "island time" meant. It wasn't measured by the clock or the calendar or even by the seasons, only by the sun and the moon. Time flowed like a golden, endless river and you simply went with the flow. Things got done—eventually, and if they didn't, what did it really matter? What mattered was that the sun rose every day, that there were fish in the sea and breadfruit on the trees.

But Nicole couldn't forget that beyond the island there was another world that clanked and bustled along in exact, measured time. She had obligations to meet in that world and couldn't stay on Saint Sophia indefinitely. This knowledge pressed more heavily upon her with each passing day.

She hadn't done much research work during her visit, or at least not on the project she'd planned to work on. Instead, she'd been investigating the legend of the Flaming Sails. Island records had verified that many locals with Indian ancestors named their first-born son Miguel. Those she interviewed had no idea why, only that it was tradition. The legend itself had been lost to them, or remembered only vaguely. It seemed that only Anabella Roseau knew the finer details of it. Or cared about it.

Nicole was alone at the patio table, pouring over the notes she'd taken during her visit with Anabella, when Greg came around the bougainvillea hedge.

"So there you are," he said. "You were supposed to meet me at the dock half an hour ago, sweetheart." He took her diving with him every day now. They'd worked out a perfect underwater relationship.

"Oh, I'm sorry, Greg." Nicole glanced at her bare wrist. She'd gotten out of the habit of wearing a watch.

"It doesn't matter," he said, bending to kiss her. His cheek knocked against her horn-rimmed glasses. "I didn't know you wore specs."

"Just for reading." She snatched them off self-consciously, sure that she looked much better without them.

"So do I," he said, sitting down beside her.

"You?" Nicole laughed. "I can't picture you with a pair of reading glasses perched on your nose."

"You forget that I used to be a staid history professor in another life." He picked up her glasses and slipped them on. "See? They suit me, don't they?"

In fact, she adored the studious demeanor the glasses gave him. "Do you ever miss teaching?" she asked.

"Sure I do. I never really intended to give it up." He carefully placed her glasses back on the table. "It's funny how life never turns out the way you planned it to. When Don Pedro came into mine, he changed everything."

"Because you wanted him to," Nicole said. "You didn't have to *act* upon the information you dug up. You could have simply written a monograph that would have been lauded by all your associates in the history department. That's what a normal person would have done. Instead, you gave up everything and became a treasure hunter."

"And in your opinion that was a crazy thing to do."

Nicole shook her head. "You were born in the wrong century," she answered. "You should have lived during a time when men could explore new worlds and have heroic quests. You had to create your own quest." She reached out and ran her hand through his thick, dark hair. "You're a romantic fool, Gregory Chase."

"Oh, well, that I may be," he answered, not sounding terribly concerned about it. "Let's go diving, Nickie."

"The same area?"

"No, it's time I gave up on it and started exploring another Carib site. This one will be number thirteen."

"Sounds lucky," Nicole commented drolly. "Listen, Greg, I've been thinking—"

He chucked her chin. "Didn't Anabella warn you that you do too much of that?"

"She told me a lot of gibberish that day we visited her."

Greg frowned. "You're having doubts about the validity of the legend?"

"No. Madame Roseau convinced me that it was authentic, even if nothing else about her is. I know enough about legends to recognize the genuine article when I hear it." She put on her glasses again and picked up her notebook. "While reviewing my notes, it occurred to me that you might be going about your search the wrong way." She glanced up, concerned that he might be offended by her interference.

He looked genuinely interested. "Go on," he said.

"Well, it makes sense to explore waters off each of the old Carib village sites, but what doesn't make sense is to go about it randomly. You could be searching forever at that rate. I think we should try to pinpoint the most likely land site first and then explore the off-shore waters."

"But how, Nickie? Don Pedro left no clues about the location of Lanalao's village."

Nicole peered at him over her glasses and smiled. "No, but the legend does. The details of it, that is."

"Such as?"

Nicole licked her finger and turned the pages of her notebook. "Here's something. The Spanish ship that took away the reluctant Don Pedro came to the island in search of fresh water, right? And many Caribs were killed when they tried to fight off the invaders."

"Don Pedro reported all that in his official journals," Greg said a bit impatiently.

"Yes, but now I think I know the reason the Caribs threw themselves into battle. According to the legend, fresh water was precious, a rare gift from the gods. That puzzled me. Saint Sophia appears to be a very lush island."

"It is," Greg agreed. "Plantations thrive here. There's plenty of rainfall because Atlantic clouds break on the mountains."

"Yet in the legend a famine began after the Man from Another Place was taken away. Obviously their crops weren't thriving. And no mountains were mentioned in the legend. Lanalao stood on the shore when she chanted. If there had been a mountain handy, it seems likely that she would have gone to the top of it to chant. It would give her a long-range view of the sea. And here's another thing." Nicole turned another page. "When Lanalao nursed the Man from Another Place, she had him drink from a magical clay bowl. In those days the island Indians drank from gourds, not clay bowls. But this particular group must have been potters. So now we know what to look for."

"Fragments of clay pots?" Greg smiled indulgently.

"No, Greg. The clay itself. Lanalao's village was located in an area that had little rainfall, with poor, clay soil. We can infer that it was a coastal location without mountains, where vegetation struggled to grow. How many sites marked on that old map meet those qualifications?"

"Not that many."

"So that narrows it down, doesn't it?"

Greg said nothing for a moment. He simply stared at Nicole. And then he stood up, yanked her out of her chair, grasped her by the waist and twirled her around. "You're brilliant!" he shouted. He put her down gently and kissed her over and over again. "There is nothing more sexy than a brilliant woman," he murmured.

"You're steaming up my glasses," she said with a sigh.

Nicole and Greg explored Saint Sophia together for three days, hiking through areas accessible only on foot. Nicole adored every minute of it, the weight of a pack on her back, the lightness of adventure in her heart, her man by her side. Her temporary man, she kept correcting herself. She had less than a week left with him before her scheduled speaking engagements began.

They found three sites that fitted the criteria of her theory, and Greg asked her to choose the one they should anchor off first. She dragged him back to each one again and stood on the shore, eyes closed, trying to get some sense of Lanalao's presence. Greg kidded her about her "scientific approach." Nicole didn't care. She was beginning to understand that there were times for rational thinking, and times for a little bit of magic.

"This one," she said at the third location, her toes curling up in the sand.

"Okay, sweetheart. I'll go by your instincts," Greg agreed, wrapping his arms around her from behind.

Nicole leaned her head against his chest. "What will you do after you find the treasure, Greg?"

"Probably return to the States and teach again. But I don't like to think about the future," he replied. "It leads to disappointments."

She knew all about disappointments. "Like you, I was once engaged to be married," she said, not quite sure why she'd mentioned it now.

"I know," Greg replied. "Your aunt told me about the bastard."

"Miles wasn't that. He had many good qualities. At least, that's the way I like to remember him. But the idea of settling down seemed to unsettle him." Nicole laughed without humor. "Everything changed after we became engaged. At times I would catch him looking at me with such a strange look in his eyes. Rather like a trapped animal. And then he would act cold, even cruel to me. Never physically. It was much more subtle than that. I would walk around with my stomach in knots and flinch every time he got that look in his eyes because I knew he would soon say something hurtful. But I couldn't let go. I thought I loved him. He was the one who finally walked out, and I was amazed how relieved I felt. I promised myself that I would never be a fool for love again."

"I'm sorry, Nickie." Greg kissed the top of her head and pressed her closer against his chest. "I'm sorry you were hurt like that. But it could have been worse. You could have married the ba—uh, Miles."

She laughed again, without bitterness. "I was so sure he was the only man in the world for me."

Greg turned her around to face him. "I hope I've changed your mind about that."

She gazed into his eyes. She saw kindness and concern and desire in their sea-green depths. But of course, unlike Miles, he didn't feel trapped. And she would never, ever make him feel that way, she promised herself. "You've given me such joy these last few weeks," she told him.

"I would never want to hurt you. Ever," Greg said, his voice low with intensity.

She lifted her hands to his face, his beloved face. "I know." And she was sure that he would never intentionally hurt her. She forced a smile. "But why are we standing here talking when we could be diving for treasure?"

He smiled back, as if relieved. "So you think this is the area where the Flaming Sails went down, do you?"

"I feel it in my bones," she assured him. "I can almost smell the masts burning."

They were diving together a few hours later, less than half a mile offshore. Greg had cautioned Nicole not to be too hopeful that they would find anything the first day, the first week, or even the first month. She hadn't reminded him that she wouldn't be around that long.

He hadn't put a damper on her high expectations, though. Her sixth sense told her they would discover something important during their dive. The water was extremely clear in this area and she could see for over a hundred feet. Beyond that distance the view was hazy but she could discern a dark mass, which could have been a rock formation. Or a hill of ballast rock! Containing her excitement, she touched Greg's shoulder and pointed. He nodded and they swam together toward the dark form.

The closer they got, the more Nicole was convinced that they had come upon the remains of a wreck. Once they reached their goal, there could be no doubt about it. The pile of rocks, about ten feet high and the length and width of a basketball court, could be nothing but the ballast put in the hold of a galleon to steady it. The wooden body of the ship itself had decayed long ago.

Nicole heard the whistle and rattle of her breathing through her regulator and tried to steady it as she poked around the rocks with Greg. When they spotted the coral-encrusted anchor they locked eyes through their face masks and for a moment wordlessly, totally connected.

They fanned away sand at the base of the rock pile for what could have been minutes or hours. Nicole had lost all concept of time. Then Greg pulled his knife from its sheath and chipped at a coral clump, dislodging what appeared to be a lump of coal. But Nicole knew better. It was a mass of sulfided silver coins. Unlike gold, which remained impervious to salt water, silver oxidized in the brine. Greg had told her how to recognize it.

He'd also told her that finding sunken treasures was the next best thing to making love and now she could understand what he meant. She could barely contain her excitement and began hand-fanning the sand with great energy. But Greg tapped her shoulder and indicated that they were going up. Forgetting once again that she had promised to obey him at all times underwater, Nicole stubbornly shook her head. He pointed to his Favre-Leuba watch, then clenched his fist and pounded his chest. She nodded her assent. He wasn't acting the macho he-man but had given her the "Air supply low" sign. They kicked to the surface together.

On deck, as soon as she'd divested herself of her gear, Nicole threw herself at Greg and hugged him tightly. "We've found it!" she shouted. "We've found the Buenaventura!" She began laughing and crying at the same time.

"Calm down, calm down," he kept saying, rubbing her trembling limbs.

"But I don't want to calm down!" she cried.

He took her below, wrapped a towel around her, sat down and pulled her into his lap. "Nicole, that wreck isn't necessarily the Buenaventura," he said in his low, quiet voice, a voice which she found infuriating at that moment. Why wasn't he as excited as she was?

"Yes, it is," she insisted.

"Please listen to me, sweetheart. I've been disappointed so many times before. The signs are good. That was egg ballast, which was used on Spanish ships. But that still doesn't mean it's from *our* ship."

She liked him calling it theirs. And she was positive that it was. Nestling her cheek against his smooth, hard chest, Nicole smiled to herself. Now that they had found the Buenaventura, Greg would have no reason to stay on this island for much longer. He could come home to the States. Home to *her*.

A little voice nagged in the back of Nicole's mind— the flat little parrot voice of Anabella, predicting that Greg wouldn't find the Buenaventura for many years. Nicole ignored it. She couldn't wait to get back to the inn to tell Jane and Toby of their find. The four of them would celebrate at dinner that night and have a toast with passion punch. No, the five of them, she corrected. Of course, Marie would be included in the celebration.

There would be six at dinner that evening, Nicole realized when she and Greg returned to the Sea Rover and she saw an attractive woman pacing the veranda. Nicole immediately guessed who she was. Susan Fitzwell had arrived.

The woman waved when she spotted them crossing the lawn, then smoothed her short pink skirt over tan, shapely legs. "Greg, how wonderful to see you again! You look better than ever," she said in a loud, throaty voice that jarred the birds out of the palm trees.

It jarred Nicole, anyway.

"Hello, Suzie." Greg crossed the wide veranda and walked right into her open, waiting arms.

Nicole sized her up as a well-preserved woman of "a certain age." Although deeply tanned, her face was unlined. Face-lift, Nicole thought. She had a luxurious crop of short, glossy black hair. Bottled, Nicole decided. She mentally gave herself a little kick before she started meowing out loud. Yet even after reprimanding herself for such catty thoughts, she couldn't help noticing how ostentatious Mrs. Fitzwell's big diamond and emerald rings were as she patted Greg's back. And how her long, ruby-red fingernails looked like talons.

"Do you hate me, darling, for that nasty mention I made of you in the article I wrote?" Suzie asked Greg with husky intensity.

"Yes," he said. But he was smiling, Nicole noticed.

"Why didn't you at least call and berate me when I sent it to you?"

"Because that's what you wanted me to do, Suzie."

She stopped hugging him and stepped away. "So what have you been up to since we last crossed paths?"

"The same old thing. Looking for that sunken ship you don't think exists."

"I've been reconsidering the possibility that it does. Any new developments?"

"Not really." Greg looked over Suzie's shoulder and sent Nicole a silent message. *Don't mention what we discovered today.*

She nodded in complete understanding.

Suzie swiveled around and gave Nicole a thorough once-over. Nicole contained the urge to comb her fingers through her wet hair and pull her wrinkled top and shorts away from the damp swimsuit she wore under them. Compared to the beautifully groomed Mrs. Fitzwell, she felt sandy and salty and grubby.

"And who's your little friend, Greg?" Suzie asked.

Since Nicole was at least three inches taller than Mrs. Fitzwell, she didn't appreciate being called little. Still, she put out her hand and introduced herself.

The other woman shook hands with surprising warmth. "How pretty you are," she observed. "Are you a guest at the Sea Rover, Ms. Webster? Or a permanent resident?"

Subtle she wasn't, Nicole thought. "No, I'm not here permanently," she replied. "I'll be leaving at the end of the week."

"And I plan to stay for two." Suzie turned to Greg. "May I have that darling cottage with the four-poster bed again?"

"Sorry. Nicole's staying there now."

"Well, when she leaves I can replace her there, can't I?"

Greg shrugged. "Sure. I don't see why not, Suzie."

Nicole felt the blood drain from her face. "Excuse me," she said. "I have to... I have to..." Cry? Scream? Go into a jealous rage of the greatest magnitude? She could think of no acceptable excuse and so she walked away without another word, silently maintaining her dignity.

Five minutes after she'd returned to her cottage, Greg tapped on her screen door.

"Go away. I'm busy," she told him.

He came in anyway. "So I see." He watched her as she packed her suitcase, throwing her clothes into it without bothering to fold them.

Since he made no comment about her actions, Nicole felt it was up to her to explain them. "I'm leaving," she said. "Your new guest can have this cottage and *replace* me tonight. Will you even notice the difference?"

"Don't be ridiculous, Nicole."

"Oh, I feel pretty ridiculous right now, I assure you," she said, her voice much higher-pitched than normal. "I thought that what we've shared together meant something to you, Chase."

"It means everything to me."

"Hah! Once I leave you'll be saying that to Suzie." She punched out the name. Soo-Zee.

"How can you say such a thing? Don't you know me better than that by now?"

The hurt in his voice made her stop packing and look at him. The hurt was in is face, too. She sank onto the bed next to the open suitcase. "I'm sorry," she said. "But it hit me so hard that I would be leaving soon and that someone else would be staying in this room."

"If it bothers you so much, I won't let Suzie stay here," Greg said. "Or anybody ever again. I'll reserve this cottage just for you, sweetheart." He sat on the bed next to her and encircled her shoulders with his arm. "It'll be waiting for you anytime you want to return to Saint Sophia. I'll even put a sign over the door. Nickie's Cottage. No Trespassing."

She sniffed. "A big sign?"

"Flashing neon if you want."

She managed a little laugh. "Your generator couldn't handle it." And she couldn't handle loving a man so much on a temporary basis, she realized. How had she let this happen to her?

He shoved the suitcase off the bed to make room for them to lie down. He cradled her against him. "My love," he whispered in her ear.

She relaxed as he kissed and fondled her. She forgot everything else but the sublime pleasure he gave her. He stayed with her and loved her until the sun slid into the sea and shadowy twilight softly crept into the room.

"It's getting late," she murmured in a satisfied stupor. "We'll be late for dinner."

"Let's skip it," he said.

"No, that wouldn't be fair to Jane and Toby. Don't forget, there's a guest staying at the Sea Rover now and you're the official host."

Greg groaned. "What's Fitzwell after, I wonder?"

"You?" Nicole suggested as lightly as she could.

"No. I'm flattered that you were jealous, but to Suzie I'm no more than a fish that got away. If she ever caught me, she would probably toss me back after a while. All she really cares about is finding sunken treasure. It's the only passion we ever shared, believe me."

Nicole did believe him. Her spurt of jealousy had flared and then sputtered out after she'd realized that it was her imminent departure that had upset her more than Susan Fitzwell's arrival. A timely arrival, she thought now. "Greg, it just occurred to me—since Suzie was once your partner, would she still have a share in the treasure you find?"

"No, the partnership was completely dissolved."

"Then she isn't going to be too pleased when you announce that you've found the Buenaventura." Nicole smiled. "Why don't you announce it at dinner? I'd love to see the look on her face when you do."

"Don't jump the gun, Nickie. We're still not sure that the wreck we discovered is Don Pedro's ship."

"You're not. I am."

"I hope with all my heart you're right, sweetheart."

"What about that clump we brought up?"

"I'll have to send it to a lab and get it analyzed. It's a complicated, delicate process to separate sulfided silver coins. Let's hope they have dates on them." He paused. "The right dates. Until then, let's not say a word about it to anyone."

"Mum's the word," she promised. She raised a finger to her lips. His finger.

Alone in his cottage after dinner, Greg paced the floor. The chunk of blackened metal sat on his worktable and whenever he passed it on his trips back and forth across the room, he glanced away, feeling guilty. He'd lied to Nicole. For the first time in their relationship he'd lied to her. There was no need to send the sulfided silver to a lab. There was nothing the least bit complicated about the task that awaited him. Still he delayed, though it made no sense to put it off. He would have to find out sooner or later.

He sat down at the table and picked up a chisel. After three sharp taps, the clump fell apart. The coins revealed inside were as shiny as the day they were minted. He carefully separated them, four in all, then walked away from the table. He wasn't ready to read the markings yet.

He thought of Nicole, waiting for him in her cottage. He longed to bring good news to her. He dreaded dashing her hopes. That was why he'd lied. If the coins glittering on the table didn't have the correct dates, he didn't want to tell her. She only had a few days left on the island and he wanted them to be perfect for her. As perfect as he could make them.

He didn't want his own hopes dashed, either. He'd been through that before. Too many times before. That should have hardened him by now, dammit. He went back to the table, sat down, and put on his reading glasses. He remembered his joke about one day needing a bifocal diving mask. It didn't seem so funny to him now. He'd invested five years of his life in this search. He was nearing the age of thirty-five. Would he end up a lonely, embittered old man, one of the island "characters" that tourists liked to snap pictures of? Not a pleasant thought.

His hand shook slightly as he picked up one of the coins and examined it under the high-intensity lamp. There was a royal crest on it and it was dated 1652. He let the coin drop from his hand and stared into space with a grim expression. The Buenaventura had gone down over a hundred years before that date.

Only one thought comforted him at that moment. Nicole was waiting for him. For now, anyway. But when she returned to the States, he couldn't expect her to wait for him. He had once asked a woman to do that and now he realized how selfish his request had been. He considered asking Nicole to live with him here on the island. But that too would be supremely selfish. She had her own life, her own goals. He couldn't expect her to give up everything and devote herself to his quest. No, he decided, he had nothing to offer her but dreams. His dreams, not hers.

He left his cottage and strolled down to hers. She was sitting on the porch step, as she had been the first night they'd made love. That seemed to him a lifetime ago. It seemed as if she'd always been part of his life, his joy. It seemed impossible to imagine life without her.

"What's wrong?" she asked softly before he'd spoken a word.

"Wrong?" He pretended surprise. "Not a thing, love."

She smiled at him, accepting his answer. "I don't think I'll be able to sleep tonight. I'm too keyed up about finding the Buenaventura." She wrapped her silky white robe closer around her and hugged herself, as if to contain the excitement.

He didn't caution her again about getting her hopes up. She looked so delighted and so precious at that moment, her freshly washed hair loose around her shoulders, her eyes bright with expectation. He'd seen such a change in her since she'd come to Saint Sophia. She'd opened herself to the magic of life, rather than shut it out with well-researched disclaimers. She reminded him of a beautiful, rare flower unfolding. It would break his heart to see her fade with disappointment now.

He took her hand and pulled her to her feet. "Let's go to bed, sweetheart. You need your rest. We're going to go diving again tomorrow, don't forget."

"Don't forget! That's all I've been thinking about. I can't wait to return to the wreck site." She grasped his hand tightly. "Oh, Greg, it's so thrilling. We may find Aztec treasures tomorrow!"

"Well, maybe not tomorrow," he said.

"Then the next day. All I hope is that we can find even one piece of the treasure together. I want to be with you when that happens."

And she would be, he thought. No matter how long it took him to find his lost treasure, when he did, she would be in his heart. He leaned down and gently kissed her forehead.

"What's wrong?" she asked again, looking into his eyes.

"Nothing, sweetheart. Everything is perfect because you are." He led her inside to the gauze-draped bed.

"Uh-oh, look who's coming," Jane said to Nicole as they sunbathed on the beach.

Lying on her stomach, Nicole pushed herself up on her elbows and saw Suzie Fitzwell heading toward them. She was wearing a big straw hat with ribbon streamers and a long, flowing magenta coverup.

"There goes our peace and quiet," Jane grumbled.

But Nicole smiled and waved at Suzie. During the last few days she'd warmed up to the woman, although Suzie was the last person Nicole would have expected to like. Her voice was too loud, and her language was either sweetly gushy or as salty as a sailor's. But she had a deep, throaty, contagious laugh and entertained them every evening at dinner with stories about her adventures, or rather misadventures, as a treasure hunter. Nicole had assumed she'd inherited her wealth from her late husband, but that hadn't been the case. Mrs. Fitzwell had made her fortune as a salvager and was "damn proud of it."

"May I join you, ladies?" she shouted as she approached.

"Please do," Nicole called back.

Jane closed her book with a sharp clap. "I doubt I'll be getting much reading done now."

But her expression was pleasant enough when Suzie plopped onto the blanket beside them. "Where's your bunny, honey?" she asked Jane.

"Toby goes fishing with Gregory every morning."

"It seems odd to see you without him. I thought you two got joined at the hip when you married." Suzie chortled over her own wit. "And how goes it with you, Nicole? I'm surprised Greg didn't take you fishing with him, since he takes you diving with him every day. You should feel honored. He never took me diving, even though I pleaded with him to. Of course he never took me to bed, either, even though I pleaded with him for that, too." Suzie threw back her head and roared. "Oh, well, win some, lose some. That's what I always say."

"You're always saying *something*, that's for sure," Jane told her, maintaining her pleasant expression. She stood. "I'd better check with Marie about dinner. We're expecting four more guests today."

"Great," Suzie said. "I love to be surrounded by people."

Nicole didn't think it was so great. She'd wanted her last days with Greg to be an undisturbed idyll.

"Jane thinks I rattle on too much and I'm not especially discreet," Suzie said once she and Nicole were alone. "But I mean no harm."

"Did you mean any harm when you wrote about Greg in that travel magazine?" Nicole asked pointedly.

"Oh, I was just trying to get his goat. Listen, I gave the Sea Rover a good plug in that article, and what I said about Greg wouldn't keep tourists away. I bet some people who read it came to the inn just to check him out and see if he really was the pirate I made him out to be."

Nicole smiled to herself. She'd been one of them.

"Besides, I did say he had oodles of charm," Suzie added. She threw off her hat, got up, and shimmied out of her cover-up. The bikini she wore was even smaller than Nicole's. She must have caught Nicole's appraising glance because she grinned. "Not a bad figure for a woman who'll never see forty again, huh?"

"You're in excellent shape, Suzie," Nicole replied. And even that was an understatement.

Suzie flopped onto the blanket again. "Greg never noticed. But that's okay. I guess I wasn't his type. You and he make a very attractive couple, by the way. I told Greg the same thing yesterday. I asked, 'What's with you and Nicole? Any plans for the future?' He didn't answer me, but his eyes got that faraway look in them. You know that look?"

Nicole nodded. She knew it well.

"I call it his Buenaventura look," Suzie continued. "When I left here last year, I doubted the ship had ever existed. I thought Greg had put one over on me. But then I hired a researcher in Spain who verified most of Greg's story. Not anything about the Aztec treasure, of course. That's all conjecture on Greg's part. The thing is, he's not even searching for it to get rich. That's one of the reasons we had a parting of the ways. When and *if* he finds the treasures, he doesn't want to sell them to private collectors. He wants a museum to have them. Do you believe that?"

Nicole nodded again. Of course Greg would want to do that.

"Well, there's no profit in that, and I'm in it for the money," Suzie said bluntly. "I recently invested a lot of money in a rig with state-of-the-art search equipment, but I don't have any new leads on wrecks to explore at the moment. So yesterday I offered Greg the loan of my rig for only ten percent of the Buenaventura find. He knows a good deal when he hears one and he accepted.''

That made no sense to Nicole. Greg didn't need Suzie Fitzwell's fancy equipment to find Don Pedro's ship. He and she had done it all on their own!

''Mind if I borrow some of your lotion, Nicole?''

''I don't understand.''

Suzie pointed to the plastic bottle beside Nicole. ''Your suntan lotion. May I use some?''

Nicole tossed it to her. ''I meant I don't understand this deal you made with Greg.''

''There I go rattling off at the mouth again. All you have to know, Nicole, is that I've decided to help Greg out again. Now isn't that good news? Let's face it, darling. Greg is never going to give any woman his complete attention until he finds the Buenaventura.''

Nicole was completely confused. But she didn't dare question Suzie further. She'd promised Greg to keep their find a secret and couldn't risk giving it away.

Suzie didn't notice her silence, since she filled the air with her own gush of words. She began telling Nicole about the time she found her first wreck in Bermuda. Nicole didn't hear a word of her story.

Later in the morning, Nicole met Greg at the dock as usual. And as usual he gave her a hearty kiss, although they'd only been apart for a few hours.

''Great catch this morning,'' he told her. ''Ever eaten shark before?''

"No, but I bet I'll be eating it tonight," she replied. "Was it a big shark?"

"Big? This shark could have starred in *Jaws*, sweetheart. I had to wrestle it aboard."

She smiled. "Save that tall story for all the guests at dinner tonight. What time do you have to pick them up at the pier?"

"The seaplane's due in at one, but Toby offered to get them. We're free to go diving all day."

"We're going to find Aztec treasure today. I can feel it," Nicole said. So far all they'd found around the wreck site was cannonballs and grapeshot.

"Don't get your hopes up, Nickie."

There it was again, Nicole thought. That strange look in his eyes. "Greg, are you hiding something from me?" she asked him.

He looked away and said nothing.

Her stomach muscles clenched. "You are, aren't you? What kind of arrangement have you made with Suzie Fitzwell? She said you made a deal to use her rig and search equipment. Why would you need it if we've already found the Buenaventura?"

He swore under his breath. "Suzie talks too much."

"Tell me the truth," Nicole demanded. She couldn't bear the thought that he'd been lying to her, but she had to know why.

Greg's broad shoulders slumped. "That wreck we discovered together isn't the Buenaventura, Nickie."

"What? But how can you be so sure?"

"I didn't have to send the sulfide clump to a lab. I broke it apart myself. There were four perfectly preserved coins inside. I'll show them to you when we go back to the inn."

"Were there dates on the coins?"

He nodded. "They were minted in 1652, Nickie. Our pal Don Pedro had gone to his final reward long before then."

"But why have you kept this from me, Greg? Why have we continued to explore the wreck when you knew it wasn't the Buenaventura?"

"I wanted you to enjoy your last week here, love. You were so thrilled about our discovery, and I couldn't see the harm in letting you keep thinking it was the right one."

She was touched that Greg had cared so much about not disappointing her. But then an uncomfortable thought occurred to her. "Didn't you ever consider that you would have had to tell me the truth eventually?"

"I didn't think that far ahead, Nickie. I just wanted you to be happy while you were here."

He had no intention of thinking about her at all after she left, she realized. It was time she faced it head-on. Once she left Saint Sophia, their relationship would be over as far as he was concerned.

"I don't feel like going diving with you today, Greg," she said in a hollow voice.

"Why not? We'll explore a new site."

She shook her head. "You go alone."

"Dammit, I knew you'd be terribly disappointed."

"I'll get over it." She gave him a quick kiss on the cheek, then turned and walked down the dock. He didn't follow her. She hadn't expected him to. She heard him start up the motor of his boat. She didn't look back. She walked up the beach toward the inn, and only when she heard the boat head for the open sea did she turn and wave goodbye.

Chapter Fourteen

What to you mean, Nickie's gone?''

Greg's voice, normally so low and even, boomed like thunder across the patio.

"She left with Toby half an hour ago," Jane calmly told him as she arranged a vase of flowers on the glass table. "She's taking the seaplane back to Saint Lucia and a flight to Boston from there. I wanted to go to the pier to see her off, but the Jeep would have been too crowded on the return trip with the guests."

"But she wasn't scheduled to leave until Friday."

"She said that she needed a few extra days back in Boston to prepare for her lecture tour. At least that's the excuse she gave me." Jane looked up from the flower arrangement and searched Greg's stricken face. "It's not like Nicole to impulsively alter her plans like that. What happened between you two this morning?''

"I disappointed her," Greg replied flatly. "Apparently she decided not to waste any more time with a man who keeps coming up empty-handed. I don't blame her. Why would an intelligent woman like Nickie want to be involved with a foolish dreamer like me?" Knowing that Jane had no answer to that, he left the patio.

He headed straight for Nicole's cottage. He still couldn't accept that she'd actually gone without saying goodbye to him. Jane could have been mistaken. Maybe Nickie hadn't left in the Jeep with Toby, after all. Maybe she'd changed her mind and was waiting in her cottage for him right now. He picked up his pace as this hope buoyed his heart, but when he threw open the screen door his heart plunged. Marie was there, about to strip the bed.

"No, don't do that!" Greg enjoined. "Leave everything the way it is."

Marie gave him a puzzled look. "But I'm getting this room ready for Madame Fitzwell. She told me she wanted to stay here after Nicole Niece departed."

"Leave it the way it is," Greg repeated evenly. "I don't want anyone else staying in this cottage."

"But what sense does that make, Greg Mister? Why should this room remain empty when we have four more guests coming in today?"

He took a deep, calming breath, not wanting to take out his frustrations on Marie. "You're right," he said. "It makes no sense. But please indulge me, Marie. We'll put all the guests in the main house, and Madame Fitzwell can very well stay where she is. If she doesn't like it, she can leave."

"Very well, if that is what you want." Marie extracted an envelope from her apron pocket. "Nicole Niece left this on the pillow. It has your name written on it, does it not?"

Greg nodded and took the envelope, feeling something bulky inside. He sank onto the bed and opened the flap, vaguely aware when he heard the screen door bang that Marie had left the room.

He'd already guessed what was inside. He took out the gold Aztec seashell he'd given Nicole. There was also a note.

> Dear Greg,
> It would be wrong for me to keep this treasure. It may bring you luck in your quest. I leave Saint Sophia with beautiful memories, but all good times must come to an end sooner or later. I thought it best to leave a few days sooner so that you could get on with your search.
>
> Best wishes, Nicole

Best wishes! Couldn't she have at least signed it *love*? He angrily tore up the note, then immediately felt sorry that he had destroyed it. It was all he had left of Nicole now. No, he had his own beautiful memories. Perhaps she had been right to leave so suddenly. Wasn't that the perfect way to end a perfect romance? No tears, no regrets.

Greg lay back and breathed in the light trace of Nicole's special scent on the pillowcase. Clutching the gold shell in his fist, he buried his face in the pillow.

* * *

One month later Nicole put in a call to the Sea Rover, praying that Greg wouldn't answer the phone. If he did, she planned to hang up, but she was still afraid of what hearing his voice again, even briefly, would do to her. She held her breath as the call went through.

"Hello, this is Mrs. Breck at the Sea Rover. May I help you?"

"Jane!" Nicole cried. Relief and disappointment clashed within her.

"Oh, Nicole, how wonderful to hear from you. How are you, dear?"

"Just fine," she lied. "I'm on the last leg of my lecture tour. I'll be speaking at the University of Vermont tomorrow, so I'm staying at your house tonight."

"Your house now," Jane corrected. "Is the furnace working all right?"

"I'm warm as toast even though it's ten below outside. Being here made me miss you so much that I couldn't resist the urge to call."

"I'm glad you did, Nicole. Frankly, I was a little worried about you. I know you've been busy traveling but I wish you'd kept in touch."

"Didn't you get my postcards?"

"Yes, but they were just short, vague notes. How are you *really*, dear?"

"I'm fine, Jane," she said again. Considering I have a big hole in my heart, she added silently.

"Well, he isn't."

"Who?"

"Oh, for goodness sake, who do you think, Nicole? Gregory, of course. He asks me every day if I've heard from you."

"He's only being polite, Jane, inquiring about your relative. But I didn't call to talk about him. Tell me how your plans for the bird sanctuary are coming along."

"Oh, we bought the tract of land we wanted." Jane laughed. "I'm no longer a millionaire. I'd rather have the sanctuary than the money, though. So would Toby."

"Good. I know you'll be happy."

"How I wish I could say the same for you, dear!"

"I'm as happy as I ever was. No complaints whatsoever."

"Don't try to fool me, Nicole. I can hear it in your voice."

"Hear what? I have a little cold, that's all."

"You're in love with him, aren't you?"

How could she possibly deny it? But she couldn't allow herself to admit it, either, so she remained silent.

"He was shocked that you left without saying goodbye to him," Jane said.

"It was best that way. Clean and simple. Apparently Greg thought so, too. He made no effort to contact me when I returned to Boston."

"He has his pride, Nicole. You're the one who left *him*."

"A few days earlier than he'd expected me to, that's all. He never suggested that he wanted me to stay longer."

"Because he knew you had obligations back in the States."

"I'm sure he was relieved that I did. Greg refers to the Buenaventura as his mistress, Jane. And no flesh and blood woman can compete with her."

"I don't believe that's true."

"It is," Nicole insisted. "All Greg wanted to offer me was a beautiful, *brief* romance, and I admit I relished every moment of it. But the spell was broken when I left Saint Sophia and returned to the cold, real world. I just need a little more time to adjust and then I'll be okay. I'll forget about him."

"I don't believe that's true," Jane said again.

No, Nicole thought sadly, it wasn't.

A good crowd turned out to hear Nicole speak at the university the next evening. As she stood behind the lectern her eyes skimmed the faces in the audience. Did any of the people looking back at her realize how miserable she was? she wondered. Did they know that she was a fool? She certainly felt like one as she began her lecture. The whole point of it was to demonstrate how courting practices evolved from primitive mating rituals and superstitions and had little to do with romantic love. Yet she herself had become swept away in a romance that had left her totally devastated. Surely she of all people should have known better!

She'd given this talk many times before and managed to get through it once again. She was quite sure that no one in the audience could guess that she'd cried herself to sleep every night for the last month. Luckily her horn-rimmed glasses hid her puffy eyes. Yet even the sight of her own glasses made her want to weep. The image of Greg trying them on was one of many seared on her mind.

"In conclusion," she said in her clipped, precise voice, "romance is a cultural development that contrives to put our basic sexual . . ." She heard the auditorium door swing open and glanced to the back of the room, irritated that someone would come in at the very end of her lecture. When she saw who it was, she thought that she was hallucinating. "A cultural development," she started again, her eyes locked on Greg's as he walked down the aisle toward the stage. "One that contrives to put our basic sexual needs on an artificial level, resulting in modern-day confusion and disappointment.

He leaped onto the stage and took her in his arms. "Hogwash," he whispered.

"What on earth are you doing here, Chase?"

"What I'm about to do is kiss you, Nickie."

Oh, to hear him call her that again! To feel his arms around her again! The rest of the world fell away as his lips met hers. She wrapped her arms around his waist and pressed him close, cherishing him. As her heart pounded to the beat of a wild Carib drum she was dimly aware that the audience was applauding.

"What are you doing here?" she asked Greg again as they walked across the icy parking lot to her car.

"Jane mentioned you were giving a talk tonight and I wanted to hear it. Sorry I was late. Flight delays. And then I had to wait forever to rent a car at the airport."

"You came all the way from Saint Sophia to hear me give a talk in Vermont?" It was below freezing and she became aware that he was only wearing a light sweater. She took off her long, woolly scarf. "Here, put this on," she told him. "Have you gone crazy, Greg?"

"I've been missing you like crazy, that's for sure."

She slipped on a patch of ice and he caught her arm to steady her. They had reached her car. She fumbled in her purse for her keys, took them out and dropped them. "I'm in a state of shock," she said.

He picked up her car keys. "Then I'd better drive you back to Jasper. I'll leave my rental here and pick it up tomorrow." He unlocked the passenger door for her, and she got in without protesting. Her head was spinning. She couldn't possibly drive.

She stared through the windshield without blinking and watched Greg go around to the driver's side, her scarf loosely wrapped around his neck. She reconsidered the possibility that she could be hallucinating. When he got in beside her and started the motor she thought she could smell the scent of sunshine and sea. She was sure she could feel the warm, gentle island breeze, then realized it was only the car heater.

"I can't believe you're really here," she told him. She could barely speak, barely form the words. Her lips were numb and she could still taste his kiss on them.

"Oh, I'm here, all right. Did you think you could just walk out of my life like that?" He stared at her intently. "You were cruel to leave me that way, Nickie."

"I didn't mean to be cruel. I wanted to make it as easy as possible for both of us to end the relationship."

"There's nothing easy about our relationship," he said. "There never has been. We still have plenty to settle between us, sweetheart."

Her poor heart skipped a beat. "Like what?"

He grinned. That insufferable, self-assured grin that she adored. "Well, for one thing, we struck it rich, diving buddy. I salvaged a lot more silver coins around that wreck we discovered together."

"How amazing!" Nicole raised her hands to her face. "That was Anabella's prophecy. She said you would find the treasure you're seeking, but it wouldn't be the one you were looking for."

"The Saint Sophian government gets twenty-five percent of the find," Greg continued. "That leaves us about a hundred thousand dollars to split down the middle."

"I can't accept money from you, Greg."

"Why not? It's only fair. Your theory and instincts led us to that wreck."

"But it turned out to be the wrong one, which discounts my input. Finding it was an accident. You salvaged the coins by yourself, and I would never expect you to split them with me, Greg."

"Okay," he easily agreed. "I won't split with you, Nickie. I'll ask you to marry me, instead."

With that he drove out of the parking lot.

She was unable to speak until they'd traveled for at least ten miles. "You want to get married?"

"The question, love, is do you?"

"I never allowed myself to even consider the possibility," she replied.

"Of getting married?"

"No. Of marrying *you*."

"Well, thanks a lot!" He kept his eyes on the road.

"Oh, Greg, you're the most wonderful lover a woman could hope for. And you're kind. And you're intelligent. And . . . and . . . I'm hopelessly in love with you." Nicole felt a great relief admitting this to both him and herself. The weight pressing down on her heart lifted the moment she did. Then she felt it press down again. "But—"

"No buts about it, Nickie. I'm in love with you, too. And I don't want to lose you again."

Tears sprang to her eyes. His words filled her with joy, but also misgivings. "Marriage means responsibilities, Greg. I would like to have children when I marry."

"Well, so would I, sweetheart. And I want to offer you more than dreams. I don't expect you to spend your life chasing after them with me in the Caribbean. I've decided to give up my search for the Buenaventura and go back to teaching."

"I can't let you give up your quest for me, Greg. One day you'll look at me with regret in your eyes and I couldn't bear that."

"That would never happen, love."

She shook her head. "No, Greg," she said. "I can't marry you."

"I didn't travel all the way up here to hear you say that, Nickie. Obviously I made a mistake." He pulled the car to the side of the road and stopped. "I should never have made the mistake of asking you to marry me while I was driving. That's not romantic at all."

He sprinkled kisses over her damp cheeks, her eyelids, the curve of her neck. "The moment you left me I realized how empty my life was before you came into it,'' he told her. He cupped her face in his palms and gazed into it. ''*You* are the treasure I've been seeking all my life, Nicole Webster. You are the rarest, most precious treasure I ever hoped to find.''

Nothing he could have said would have meant more to her than that. Still, when he lowered his face she turned hers away. ''Please don't kiss me again,'' she pleaded. ''I need to think.''

He dropped his hands from her face and groaned. ''Didn't Anabella warn you about thinking too much?''

''Just give me a minute. My head hasn't stopped spinning since you came back into my life.''

''I'll give you longer than that.'' Greg put the car into gear. ''I'll give you as much time as you need, Nickie.''

He didn't say another word during the drive back to Jasper. Nicole only said a few—to give him directions to the house. When he stopped in front of it she cleared her throat.

''I've come up with a compromise, Greg.''

''I don't like the sound of that,'' he said. ''I want you to marry me, Nickie.'' He hit his fist against the steering wheel for emphasis.

She covered his fist with her soft hand. ''Oh, I'll marry you, my love,'' she assured him. ''But only if you agree to one condition.''

''Which is?''

''That we'll return to Saint Sophia every summer to search for the Buenaventura. We'll keep going back until we find it.'' She paused. ''Together.''

''Agreed,'' he said in a thick voice. ''Together.''

"I'd like to get married in the same church Jane and Toby did."

Greg nodded. "We'll call them tonight and tell them to get up to Vermont as soon as possible."

But when they entered the house they forgot all about calling Jane and Toby. They went straight upstairs instead and became lost in their love for each other. Much later the next morning they placed a call to Saint Sophia and announced the good news. Nobody at the Sea Rover seemed especially surprised to hear it.

* * * * *

COMING NEXT MONTH

#601 LOVE FINDS YANCEY CORDELL—Curtiss Ann Matlock
Yancey Cordell had every reason to be cynical about Annalise Pardee. Yet the fragile new ranch owner inspired a strange kind of loyalty...and evoked something suspiciously like love.

#602 THE SPIRIT IS WILLING—Patricia Coughlin
Thrust into an out-of-body experience, Jason Allaire landed the unlikely role of guardian angel to adorable oddball Maxi Love. But would earthy masculine urges topple his halo and destroy his second chance at love?

#603 SHOWDOWN AT SIN CREEK—Jessica St. James
LaRue Tate wasn't about to let the government commandeer her precious prairieland. But when "government" fleshed out as handsome, rakish J. B. Rafferty, she faced an unexpected showdown—with her own bridling passions!

#604 GALAHAD'S BRIDE—Ada Steward
Horseman Houston Carder had a heart the size of Texas, with more than enough room for sheltering delicate Laura Warner. But this particular damsel seemed to resist rescue, no matter how seductive the Sir Galahad!

#605 GOLDEN ADVENTURE—Tracy Sinclair
The thrill of being romanced by a mysterious expatriate made it worth missing her boat. Or so thought stranded traveler Alexis Lindley...until she discovered the dashing adventurer was a wanted man.

#606 THE COURTSHIP OF CAROL SOMMARS—Debbie Macomber
Cautious Carol Sommars successfully sidestepped amorous advances—until her teenage son rallied his best buddy, who rallied *his* sexy single dad, whose fancy footwork threatened to halt the single mom's retreat from romance....